# THERAPY

# ALSO BY SEBASTIAN FITZEK

# SEBASTIAN FITZEK

## THERAPY

Translated from the German
by Sally-Ann Spencer

HEAD
*of* ZEUS

*An Aries Book*

First published in Germany as *Die Therapie*
in 2006 by Knaur Taschenbuch

First published in the English language in 2008 by Pan Books

This edition published in the UK in 2023 by Head of Zeus,
part of Bloomsbury Publishing Plc

9 7 5 3 2 4 6 8

A catalogue record for this book is available from the British Library.

ISBN (PB): 9781837933556
ISBN (E): 9781837933563

Printed and bound in Great Britain by
CPI Group (UK) Ltd, Croydon CR0 4YY

Head of Zeus
First Floor East
5–8 Hardwick Street
London EC1R 4RG

WWW.HEADOFZEUS.COM

*For Tanja Howarth*

# Prologue

As the thirtieth minute ticked by, he knew he would never see his daughter again. Josephine had opened the door, glanced round briefly and slipped inside the old man's office. At twelve years old, his baby girl was gone forever. He knew it with dreadful certainty. There would be no more smiles as he scooped her up and carried her to bed; no more waiting for her to fall asleep so he could switch off her bedside lamp; no more waking in the night, shaken from his dreams by her agonized screams.

The realization was devastating and sudden, hitting him with the force of a speeding truck.

Viktor Larenz stood up clumsily, but his legs seemed to cling to the seat, warning him not to rely on their support. He imagined himself toppling to the scuffed wooden floor and lying prone in the waiting room, slotted between the plump housewife with psoriasis and the coffee table piled high with ancient magazines. He felt like fainting, but even that small mercy was denied him. His mind was still alert.

*Patients will be seen according to the SERIOUSNESS of their condition, NOT in order of arrival.*

He stared at the padded leather door, the lettering on the sign swimming before his eyes.

Dr Grohlke, an allergy specialist, was a family friend and the twenty-second doctor on Viktor's list. So far, twenty-one doctors had drawn a blank with Josy. The cause of her illness had baffled them all.

The first, an emergency physician, had been called out on Boxing Day, exactly eleven months previously, to the family home in Schwanenwerder. Josephine had vomited in the night and was suffering from diarrhoea. Initially they assumed it was an upset stomach brought on by the three-cheese Christmas fondue, but eventually Isabell called their private health-care line while Viktor carried their daughter in her light cambric nightdress to the lounge. He could remember how frail her arms had seemed, one hooked around his neck, hugging him for support, the other clutching her favourite toy, a fluffy blue cat called Nepomuk. Under the rigorous gaze of the assembled relatives, the doctor listened to her bony chest, administered an electrolyte infusion and prescribed a homoeopathic drug.

'Gastro-enteritis. It's doing the rounds, I'm afraid. It'll sort itself out in no time. She'll be back on her feet by the end of the week.' With that, the doctor took his leave. *It'll sort itself out.* They should never have believed him.

Viktor came to a halt outside Dr Grohlke's door. The metal handle was stiff, refusing to yield to the pressure he applied. Had the strain of the past few hours reduced him to this? He wondered at his own feebleness, then realized that the door was locked. *Locked from the inside.*

Why would anyone lock the door?

He spun around, seeing the room in a series of frozen images that presented themselves to his consciousness like the pages of a flip book, jerky and delayed: framed photos of Ireland on the walls, a rubber tree languishing in a dusty corner by the window, the psoriasis patient, still waiting to be seen. He gave the handle a final furious shake and stumbled out of the waiting room into the corridor and towards the impossibly crowded foyer. Anyone would think Grohlke was the only doctor in Berlin.

Viktor advanced towards the desk. First in line was a spotty-faced teenager, presumably waiting for a prescription, but Viktor swept past him. He knew the receptionist from previous visits and was relieved to see her at the desk. Half an hour earlier, when he and Josy had arrived at the surgery, a stranger had been standing in for her, but now Maria was back at the helm. She was in her early twenties and as solid as a goalkeeper, but she had a daughter of her own. He could count on her support.

'I need you to unlock the office,' he demanded in a voice more strident than he had intended.

'Good morning, Dr Larenz. Nice to see you again.' Maria was quick to recognize the psychiatrist. He hadn't been to the clinic in a while, but she was accustomed to seeing his face in magazines and on TV. Good looks,

3

combined with a knack for explaining psychological problems in a straightforward way, made him a popular guest on chat shows. On this occasion, the famously eloquent Dr Larenz was failing to make much sense.

'I demand to see my daughter!'

The adolescent stared at the man who had elbowed his way to the front of the queue and, sensing a problem, took a step back. Maria seemed flustered but strove to maintain her receptionist's smile.

'I'm afraid I don't follow, Dr Larenz,' she said, tugging on her left eyebrow where her piercing would normally be. She always fiddled with the silver barbell when nervous, but at Dr Grohlke's request, she removed it for work. He took an old-fashioned pride in appearances.

'Does Josephine have an appointment?'

Viktor opened his mouth, ready to unleash a furious tirade, then thought better of it and kept quiet. Of course they had an appointment. Isabell had rung the practice, and he had chauffeured Josy to the clinic; the usual routine.

'Dad, what's an allergist?' Josy had asked him in the car. 'Is it something to do with the weather?'

'No, honey, you're thinking of meteorologists.' He watched her in the rear-view mirror and wished he could stroke her blonde hair. She seemed incredibly fragile, like an angel sketched on Japanese silk.

'Allergists look after people who get sick when they come into contact with certain substances.'

'Is that what's wrong with me?'

'Maybe.' *Let's hope so*, he added to himself. Any diagnosis would be a start. Josephine's illness and her mysterious symptoms had taken control of their lives. Six months had elapsed since she last attended school: her spasms were too distressing and sudden for her to sit in a classroom with her peers. For Isabell, it meant working part-time in order to oversee Josy's home-schooling. Viktor, in the meantime, had shut down his Friedrichstrasse practice and was caring for his daughter or, more accurately, his daughter's doctors. The last few weeks had disappeared in an endless round of appointments and consultations, for which they had nothing to show. No one could make sense of Josy's seizures, her susceptibility to infection or her night-time nosebleeds. Every now and then the symptoms abated or vanished for a while, long enough for the family to gather hope, but then the sickness would return – in most cases, more vigorously than before. So far the physicians, haematologists and neurologists had succeeded only in ruling out cancer, Aids, hepatitis and a host of diseases. One doctor had even run tests for malaria. The results came back clear.

'Dr Larenz?'

Maria's voice cut through his thoughts, pulling him back to the clinic. He realized he had been staring at her open-mouthed.

'What have you done with her?' His voice returned to him suddenly, each word sounding louder than the last.

'I'm sorry, Dr Larenz, but I don't quite . . .'

'What have you done with *Josy*?'

The chattering patients fell silent as Viktor's question echoed through the room. It was obvious from Maria's expression that she was wondering what to do. Erratic behaviour was only to be expected at the clinic: Grohlke's doors were open to anyone who cared to make an appointment, and the practice was situated only a stone's throw from the prostitutes and junkies in Lietzenburger Street. On occasions, it seemed as if the red-light district had relocated to the lobby, and Maria would find herself dealing with undernourished rent boys who didn't give two hoots about eczema but needed a fix.

Dr Viktor Larenz presented a predicament of an entirely different kind. For a start, he wasn't clad in dirty track pants or wearing a T-shirt riddled with holes. His face was free from oozing pimples and his feet were too elegant for battered trainers. In fact, there was something undeniably distinguished about his trim build, upright posture, broad shoulders, high forehead and assertive chin. A Berliner by birth and upbringing, he was frequently mistaken for a patrician from the north, and it was only his lack of greying temples and a classical nose that prevented him from appearing the perfect Hanseatic gentleman. Even so, there was something suavely appealing about his curly brown hair, which he had taken to wearing longer, and crooked nose, a painful reminder of a sailing accident. He was forty-three years old, but his age was indeterminate and his appearance left little doubt that this was a man whose handkerchiefs were monogrammed and who never carried change. His skin was perhaps a little pallid, but that was the hallmark of a high-flying doctor with a busy career. All this served to heighten Maria's dilemma. Distinguished psychiatrists who spent a small fortune on tailor-made suits had a natural aversion to making spectacles of themselves, but Dr Viktor Larenz was shouting hysterically and waving his arms. Maria, unable to make sense of the outburst, had no idea what to do.

'Larenz!'

Viktor turned in the direction of the gravelly voice. Alarmed by the disturbance, Dr Grohlke, a gaunt old man with sandy hair and hollowed eyes, had excused himself from his consultation and emerged from his office. His expression conveyed concern.

'Is something the matter?'

The enquiry seemed to stoke Viktor's wrath. 'What have you done with Josy?'

Dr Grohlke shrank back in alarm. He had known the Larenz family for almost ten years but he had never seen Viktor like this.

'Listen, Larenz, old chap, why don't you come into my office and we can . . .'

But Viktor was no longer listening. His eyes were fixed on the door to the office, which the allergist had left ajar. He took off at a run, sending the door flying open with his foot. It crashed into a trolley holding instruments and jars. The woman with psoriasis was lying on a couch. Her upper body was exposed, and in the shock of the moment she forgot to cover her breasts.

'What's the matter with you, Larenz!' shouted Dr Grohlke, but Viktor was out of the room and running down the corridor.

'Josy!'

He doubled back, trying every door.

'Josy! Where are you?' His voice cracked with panic.

'Dr Larenz, please!'

The elderly physician hurried after him as best he could, but Viktor, out of his mind with anxiety, was deaf to his pleas.

'What about this room?' he demanded when the final door on the left refused to yield.

'Cleaning products. Nothing but cleaning products. The cleaner looks after the key.'

'Open up!' Viktor shook the handle like a man possessed.

'Now look here . . .'

'OPEN UP!'

Dr Grohlke seized his arms and gripped them with surprising strength.

'Calm down, Larenz! You've got to listen to me. Your daughter isn't in that cupboard. The cleaner locked it first thing this morning and she won't be back till tomorrow.'

Viktor's breath came in gasps. He listened to the words without absorbing their meaning.

'Let's deal with this logically.' Dr Grohlke relaxed his grip and laid a hand on Viktor's shoulder.

'When did you last see your daughter?'

'Half an hour ago,' Viktor heard himself say. 'I left her in the waiting room and she went into your office.'

The old man shook his head in consternation and glanced at Maria, who had followed them out of the foyer.

'I haven't seen Josephine,' she told her boss. 'She wasn't booked in for today.'

*Nonsense!* Viktor wanted to scream at her. He clutched his head.

'I know for a fact that Isabell made the appointment. We arrived here this morning before Maria started work. The fellow at reception told us to go through and wait. Josy was tired and frail, so I went to fetch her some water, and by the time I got back she was—'

'Fellow?' queried Grohlke. 'The support staff are women.'

Viktor looked at him disbelievingly, still grappling with what he was hearing.

'I haven't set eyes on Josy all morning. She didn't have an appointment.'

The doctor's words were all but obliterated by a high-pitched noise that reached Viktor's ears from a distance, becoming louder and more oppressive as it drew near.

'Haven't seen her?' he said distraughtly. 'Of course you've seen her. I was on my way back from the water fountain when the man at reception called her through. I'd promised Josy that she could see you on her own. She's twelve now and she likes a bit of independence –

she even locks the bathroom door. In any case, when I got back and she wasn't in the waiting room, I assumed she was with you.'

It dawned on Viktor that he had failed to say a single word. His mouth was open and his mind was racing, but the thoughts were trapped inside his head. He looked around helplessly, feeling as though the world was slowing down. The noise became more piercing, more intolerable, until he could barely hear the hubbub around him. Everyone seemed to be addressing him at once: Maria, Dr Grohlke, even some of the patients.

'I haven't seen Josy for nearly a year.' That was the last statement that Viktor heard with any clarity. For a fleeting moment, everything became apparent. Like a dreamer on the cusp of waking, he glimpsed the awful truth. For a fraction of a second the whole business was laid open: Josy's illness and the pain that had haunted her for the past eleven months. He knew what had happened, knew what had been done to her and, with a lurching stomach, knew they would be after him too. Sooner or later they would get to him, he knew it with unshakeable conviction, but the moment passed and the horrible truth escaped him, disappearing as forlornly as a single drop of water in a flood.

Viktor raised his hands to his head. The piercing noise was getting closer all the time, agonizing and overwhelming, more than he could bear. It sounded like the shriek of a tortured animal, not a human cry, and it ended some time later, when his mouth eventually closed.

# 1

*Years later*

He could never have foreseen that he might one day change places. At one time the room he was in, a spartan private ward at Berlin-Wedding Psychosomatic Clinic, had been reserved for his most difficult patients, but now eminent psychiatrist Dr Viktor Larenz found himself strapped to the narrow hydraulic bed, legs and arms tied down with grey elastic straps.

Not a single person had visited in all the time he had been there – no friends, former colleagues or family. The only distraction, besides the yellowing woodchip paper, grease-spotted brown curtains and water-stained ceiling, was the twice-daily appearance of Dr Martin Roth, a young consultant psychiatrist at the clinic. No one had actually requested a visitor's permit, not even Isabell. Dr Roth had explained the situation, and Viktor could scarcely blame his former wife. Not after what had happened.

'How long has it been since you stopped my meds?'

The psychiatrist paused his examination of the electrolyte drip hanging from a three-pronged metal stand at the head of Viktor's bed. 'Three weeks, Dr Larenz.'

It was, Viktor felt, to Roth's credit that he continued to address him by his title. Over the last few days they had conducted a number of conversations and Roth always treated him with absolute respect.

'How long have I been lucid?'

'Nine days exactly.'

'Right.' Viktor paused for a moment. 'So when will I be released?'

The quip brought a smile to Dr Roth's face. They both knew that he would never be discharged. If he ever left the clinic, it would be for another psychiatric facility of similar security.

Viktor gazed down at his hands and shook the straps lightly. The clinic had obviously learned from experience. He had been stripped of his belt and shoelaces as soon as he was admitted. There was no mirror in the bathroom, and during his twice-daily supervised trips to the toilet he had no means of seeing whether he looked as wretched as he felt. At one stage in life he had been complimented on his appearance, attracting attention because of his broad shoulders, thick hair and well-toned body, perfect for a man of his age. These days his declining physique left little to be admired.

'Tell me truthfully, Dr Roth: how does it feel to see me lying here like this?'

The psychiatrist, mindful to avoid eye contact, stooped to pick up the clipboard at the foot of the bed. He seemed to be debating what to say. *Pity? Concern?*

He decided on the truth: 'Alarming.'

'Because the same thing might happen to you?'

'I suppose that strikes you as selfish.'

'No, just honest. I appreciate your frankness. Besides, I'm not surprised that you feel that way. We have a good deal in common, after all.'

Roth merely nodded.

Present circumstances notwithstanding, the two men's lives were alike in many ways. They had both enjoyed privileged childhoods in the sheltered environment of Berlin's elegant boroughs: Viktor, descended from a long line of corporate lawyers, in Wannsee, and Roth, the child of two hand surgeons, in Westend. After studying medicine at Berlin's Free University, they had gone on to specialize in disorders of the mind. As the sole beneficiaries of their parents' wills, they had come into possession of the family estate and a sizeable fortune – but instead of retiring for the rest of their days, they had ended up in the clinic as patient and doctor, brought together by coincidence or fate.

'You can't deny there's a certain similarity between us,' said Viktor. 'So what would you have done if you were me?'

'You mean, if it were *my* daughter and I found out who put her through such pain...' Roth finished his notes, replaced the clipboard and allowed himself to meet Viktor's gaze. 'To be honest, I don't think I'd survive what you had to cope with.'

Viktor laughed uncertainly. 'I didn't. It killed me. Death can be unimaginably cruel.'

'Perhaps you could tell me about it.' Roth perched on the edge of Viktor's bed.

'About what?' He needn't have asked. Viktor knew exactly what the psychiatrist was suggesting. They had discussed the matter several times before.

'All of it. I want you to tell me the whole story: what happened to Josephine, what was making her ill . . . Why don't you tell me what happened and start from the beginning?'

'You've heard most of it already.'

'I'd like to hear the details. I want to know step by step what happened and why it ended that way.'

*The final catastrophe.*

Viktor allowed the air to escape from his lungs and stared at the patchy ceiling. 'The awful thing is, during all those years after Josy disappeared, I thought nothing could be worse than not knowing. Four whole years without a reported sighting, with no reason to believe she was alive. Sometimes I longed for the phone to ring and a voice to tell me that her corpse had been found. I thought nothing could be more agonizing than being in limbo, never knowing, just suspecting. But I was wrong. There is something worse.'

Roth waited for him to continue.

'The truth is worse.' His voice was almost a whisper. 'The truth. I almost glimpsed it at the start. It came to me while I was standing in Dr Grohlke's clinic on the day that Josy disappeared. It was so dreadful, so unbearable that I had to shut it out. Much later it caught up with me again and this time I couldn't ignore it. It came after me and confronted me; quite literally confronted me. It stared me in the face.'

'What happened?'

'I found myself face to face with the person responsible and it was too much to bear. Well, you know better than most what happened on the island and what became of me after that.'

'The island,' said Roth musingly. 'Parkum, wasn't it? What took you there?'

'You're the psychiatrist; you tell me.' Viktor smiled. 'Very well, I'll give you my version of the answer. A news magazine requested an exclusive interview. I'd been approached by the press more times than I can remember and I'd always turned them down. Isabell didn't like the idea of talking to the media. Then *Bunte* emailed me some questions and I started to wonder: perhaps doing the interview would straighten out my thoughts. I wanted closure.'

'And you thought Parkum would be the place to work on your response?'

'Yes.'

'Did anyone go with you?'

'My wife was against the idea. She had an important business appointment in New York and didn't want to come. Frankly, I was glad of the solitude. I hoped Parkum would give me the space I needed.'

'The space to say goodbye to your daughter.'

It was a statement, not a question, but Viktor nodded

all the same. 'Yes, I suppose you could call it that. In any case, I loaded the car, put the dog in the back, and drove to the coast. We caught the car ferry to Sylt, then a passenger boat to Parkum. If only I'd known what was in store for me, I wouldn't have gone.'

'Tell me about Parkum. What happened on the island? When did you start to notice the connections?'

*Josephine's mystery illness. Her disappearance. The magazine article.*

Viktor lowered his chin to his chest and rotated his head. There was a cracking sound as the vertebrae in his neck clicked into place. Any other form of movement was impossible with his limbs tied to the bed. He inhaled slowly and closed his eyes. It never took more than a few seconds for his thoughts to lead him back to Parkum; back to the thatched cottage on the beach where he had hoped, four years after the tragedy, to get his life back on track. He had searched for a new beginning and tried to find closure, but the process had cost him everything he had.

# 2

*Five days before the truth, Parkum*

> *Bunte: What was it like in the aftermath of your daughter's disappearance?*
> Larenz: Like death. Of course, I was still eating, drinking and breathing and I sometimes managed to sleep for a couple of hours at a stretch, but I wasn't living anymore. My life was over the day that Josy went missing.

The cursor lingered at the end of the line, blinking steadily at Viktor. He had been on the island for a week, getting up early and working into the night at his antique mahogany desk, trying to find an answer to the magazine's first question. That morning he had finally succeeded in typing three sentences in a row.

Like death. There was no other way of describing how he had felt in the days and weeks following Josy's disappearance.

He closed his eyes.

Viktor couldn't recall what had happened after the scene in Dr Grohlke's clinic. He had no memory of where he had gone, whom he had spoken to or how things had unfolded in the chaos that pulled his family apart. His wife had shouldered most of the burden. Isabell was the one who had searched through Josy's wardrobe and worked out what she had been wearing. She had imparted the news to family and friends and found a suitable photo, sliding it out of the cellophane of the family album to give to the police. Meanwhile, her psychiatrist husband had wandered aimlessly through the streets. Dr Viktor Larenz had faced only one truly serious crisis in his life and it had brought him to his knees. Isabell had coped much better from the start. After four months she had returned to work as a full-time management consultant, while he had sold his private practice and retired.

A high-pitched beep sounded from the laptop, signalling that the power was running low. That first morning at the house, Viktor had moved the desk away from the fireplace and positioned it in front of the window. It gave him a panoramic view of the sea, but there was nowhere to plug in a charger. If he wanted to look out over the breathtakingly beautiful wintry North Sea he had to transfer the computer every six hours to a coffee table by the hearth where the battery could recharge. He saved the Word file hurriedly before the data was lost forever.

*Lost like Josy.*

His eyes swept the surface of the sea and he turned abruptly from the window, afraid that the seething water was a mirror of his soul. A gale was blowing up, whistling over the thatched roof and whipping the waves to towering heights. There was no mistaking its meaning. November was almost over and winter, abetted by its accomplices snow and frost, was there to stake its claim.

*Death*, thought Victor as he stood up and carried the laptop to the coffee table where the charger was waiting.

The house, a small two-storeyed affair, was a 1920s construction that had survived without the attentions of a handyman since Viktor's parents died. Halberstaedt, the island's mayor, had kept the generator and electrics working, for which Viktor was especially grateful in weather like this. It was a long time since anyone in the family had stayed in the wooden cottage and it was falling into disrepair. The walls needed painting, both inside and out, and the parquet floor was long overdue for a polish, except in the hallway where the blocks were crying out to be replaced. Sun and rain had warped the frames of the double-glazed windows, making the rooms unnecessarily draughty and damp. Back in the 1980s, the decor had seemed luxurious and the family's wealth was manifest in the choice of furnishings, but the Tiffany lamps, soft leather armchairs and teak shelves had acquired a permanent coating of dust. No one had cleaned them for years.

Four years, one month and two days, to be precise.

Viktor did not need to check the tear-off calendar in the kitchen to know the date of his last visit. Just over four years had elapsed since he last set foot on Parkum. Even then, the ceiling had needed painting and the mantelpiece above the fireplace had been coated with soot for some time. In those days, though, there was a sense of overriding order.

His life had been intact.

By late October that year, the illness had sapped Josy of most of her strength, but she had still been well enough to accompany him to the cottage.

Viktor sat down on the leather couch, plugged in his laptop and tried not to think about the weekend preceding their fateful visit to the clinic. The memories flooded back.

Four years.

It was forty-eight months since Josy went missing. Despite various police campaigns, appeals by the national media and a two-part TV special, she had vanished without trace, yet Isabell maintained that their daughter was still alive. That was why she had tried to dissuade him from the interview.

'You don't need closure,' she told him as he prepared to drive away.

They were on the gravel drive outside the house and Viktor had already stowed his luggage into their black Volvo estate: three suitcases, one containing clothes and the other two for documents regarding Josy's disappearance – newspaper cuttings, transcripts, and the reports submitted by Kai Strathmann, the private investigator he had hired.

'There's nothing to come to terms with. You don't

need to say goodbye,' she insisted. 'Our daughter is alive.' She had nothing more to say on the matter, so she let Viktor go to Parkum while she took off for New York on another of her business trips. She was probably in some skyscraper on Park Avenue right now. Work was her way of distracting herself.

A burning log flared up, crackling as it disintegrated in the hearth. Viktor gave a nervous start, and Sindbad, who had been dozing under the desk, leapt to his feet and yawned reproachfully at the flames. The golden retriever was a stray, found by Isabell two years ago in the car park at Wannsee baths.

'What the hell were you thinking? You can't replace our daughter with a dog!' he had thundered at her when she came home with Sindbad. The housekeeper had scurried into the first-floor laundry in alarm.

'What are you going to call it? Joey?'

Even then Isabell had refused to be provoked. Not for nothing was she descended from one of Germany's most venerable banking dynasties and her unshakeable poise was worthy of her Hanseatic birth. Only her clear blue eyes betrayed what she was really thinking: if Viktor had taken better care of Josy, she would still be with them, jumping up and down with excitement at the prospect of owning a dog. He knew that she blamed him, even though she never said a word.

In the end, Sindbad stayed, and by an irony of fate Viktor was the one to whom he became attached.

It was time for another cup of tea. Viktor stood up and walked to the kitchen, the retriever following lazily at his heels in the hope of an afternoon snack.

'No chance, old boy!' Viktor stooped to give the dog a friendly pat and noticed that his ears were flat against his head.

'What's wrong, Sindbad?' He crouched beside it and heard something too. It was a metallic noise, a kind of scratching or grating that brought back ancient memories. *What was it?* The sound was buried in the past.

Viktor crept towards the door.

There it was again, like a coin being dragged across the floor. There was silence for a moment, and then it came back.

Viktor paused, holding his breath, as the memory took shape. It was a noise he had often heard as a child; the rasping of a metal key as it scraped against fired clay; a noise his father had made when he came home from sailing and fetched the spare key from beneath the ceramic flowerpot by the door.

It couldn't be his father.

Viktor froze. Someone knew where his parents had kept their key, and that someone was intent on coming in. Were they looking for him?

Heart thumping, he strode into the hall and peered through the spyhole in the heavy oak door. No one in sight. He was about to lift the yellowing blinds and look through the window to the right of the veranda when he changed his mind and pressed his face to the door.

Horrified, he leapt backwards. His pulse was racing. Surely he must have imagined . . .

Blood was thundering in his ears, and the hairs on his forearms were standing on end. He *knew*; he knew beyond a doubt what he had seen. For a fraction of a second a human eye had stared back at him, peering through the spyhole into the house. The eye seemed familiar to him, although he had no idea who it was.

He had to pull himself together.

Taking a deep breath, he yanked open the door.

'What the hell . . . ?' Viktor intended to frighten the unknown intruder by challenging him at the top of his voice, but he tailed off mid-sentence, surprised to find himself alone. The porch was empty and there was no one on the garden path leading to the gate, six metres from the door. The gravel road to the village was deserted. Viktor stepped outside, descended the five steps into the garden and peered beneath the veranda, where he had waited during childhood games for the neighbours' kids to find him. Now, even in the fading sunlight, it was obvious that nothing sinister was lurking in the gloom, only a few dead leaves, swept there by the wind.

Shivering slightly, Viktor rubbed his hands together as he hurried up the steps. The wind had almost succeeded in closing the oak door and it took a concerted effort to pull it open against the gusts. He was about to walk in when he stopped in his tracks.

There it was again. This time it sounded less metallic,

a little higher in pitch, and it was coming from a different direction. The noise was no longer outside the house: it was sounding from the sitting room.

The intruder was announcing his presence. Someone was inside.

# 3

Viktor inched towards the sitting room, scanning the hall for possible weapons in case the intruder was armed.

It was no use relying on Sindbad to defend him. The retriever loved people and would sooner play with strangers than chase them from the premises. Besides, the dog had already slunk away to resume his afternoon nap, leaving his master to take care of the disturbance.

'Hello?'

Silence.

Viktor knew for a fact that Parkum's last recorded break-in dated back to 1964. According to the police report, the incident was part of a drunken quarrel and no punitive measures had been taken. None of this did much to reassure him.

'Is someone there?'

He held his breath, creeping along the corridor as softly as possible. Despite his best efforts to be quiet, the ageing parquet groaned beneath his shifting weight. The leather soles of his brogues betrayed his presence with every step.

Viktor wondered why he was bothering to skulk around when seconds earlier he had shouted at full volume. He reached for the handle and was about to enter the sitting room, when the door swung open from inside. The shock was so great that he forgot to cry out.

The sight of the stranger inspired both rage and relief. On the one hand, he was relieved to see a small, attractive woman and not a hulking thug; on the other he was furious at her brazen attempt to break into his house in broad daylight.

'How did you get in?' he asked sharply. The woman stood her ground, showing neither embarrassment nor fear.

'I knocked and the back door was open. I'm sorry to disturb you.'

'Disturb me?'

Viktor's fear had vanished, replaced by an urgent need to let off steam. He rounded on the woman. 'To hell with the disturbance. The shock nearly killed me!'

'Please accept my apologies—'

'You're lying,' Viktor said curtly, pushing past her. 'I never use that door. It was locked.'

Admittedly, the door could just as well have been open, since he never checked, but he had no intention of letting her off the hook. Instead, he stationed himself beside his desk and looked her up and down. Something about his uninvited guest seemed vaguely familiar, although he was certain they had never met. Her blonde hair was arranged in a medium-length plait, and at five foot four, she was terribly thin; yet for all her skinniness she looked decidedly feminine, with wide hips and shapely breasts. If only she were a little taller she could almost have been a model. Viktor looked at her porcelain skin and shiny white teeth, half expecting her to say that she was shooting a commercial on the beach.

'I'm not lying to you, Dr Larenz. I don't make a habit of lying and I'm not about to start now.'

Viktor ran his hand through his hair and tried to collect his thoughts. The situation was absurd. The woman had broken into his house, scared him to death and now she had the nerve to contradict him: it was like a bad dream.

'I don't know who you are, but listen here: I'm ordering you to leave my house immediately. Don't even—'

He looked at the stranger intently. 'Hang on a minute. Who are you?'

He was suddenly struck by how hard it was to guess her age. At first sight she seemed young, probably in her mid-twenties judging by her flawless skin. But her clothes belonged to a woman of more mature years.

She was dressed in a pink Chanel suit and a black knee-length cashmere coat with black kid gloves, a designer handbag and perfume of a kind that Isabell would wear. She spoke with a confidence and dignity that would seem precocious in anyone less than thirty.

*Is she deaf?* wondered Viktor. She seemed not to have heard his question and remained standing at the door, staring silently from a distance.

'Well, no matter. Whoever you are, you shouldn't be in my house and you've outstayed your welcome. Be so kind as to use the front door and keep away from my property. I don't wish to be disturbed again.'

The woman took two quick paces towards him, causing him to back away.

'Don't you want to know who I am, Dr Larenz? Surely you're not going to send me away without asking why I came.'

'Indeed I am.'

'I expect you're wondering what a woman like me is doing on a godforsaken island like this.'

'No.' Suddenly Viktor felt himself waver. He had almost forgotten what it was like to take an interest in someone else.

'So you don't want to know how I tracked you down?'

'No.'

'I can tell you're interested. You may as well be honest with me.'

'Honest with you? That's rich coming from someone who's broken into my house.'

'If only you'd listen, you'd see that my condition is—'

'Irrelevant,' Larenz cut her off. 'Completely irrelevant. And if you're aware of my situation, which I'm sure you are, you'll know it's unpardonably inconsiderate to impose on me like this.'

'Your situation? I'm afraid I don't follow, Dr Larenz.'

'What?' For a moment Viktor wondered what was

more astonishing: the fact that the stranger continued to contradict him, or the honesty in her voice when she made such preposterous claims. 'Then I suppose you haven't seen a newspaper in four years.'

'I'm afraid not,' she said, not bothering to explain.

Viktor's growing bewilderment was matched by a desire to find out more. 'Surely you know that my clinic is closed. I sold the place two years ago to—'

'Professor van Druisen. Exactly. I was his patient and he referred me to you.'

'He did what?' Viktor could scarcely believe his ears. His unwanted guest had succeeded in gaining his full attention.

'It wasn't an official referral, but the professor was adamant that you were the man for my case. Quite frankly, you're my first choice too.'

Viktor shook his head slowly. Why would van Druisen divulge his private address to a patient? Surely his old mentor knew better than that. Besides, it was obvious that Viktor was in no fit state to practise, and the beach house was hardly the most appropriate setting. He would call the professor later and settle the matter with him. For the time being, his priority was to get rid of the intruder and restore a sense of order.

'I'm afraid you'll have to leave. You're wasting your time here.'

The woman made no effort to go.

Viktor's panic was slowly turning to exhaustion. With a dull sense of certainty he realized that his fears had been justified: he would not find the necessary distance to forge a new beginning. Spectres had followed him to the island; both those of the living and the dead.

'I understand that you don't want to be disturbed. Patrick Halberstroem ferried me over this morning and wouldn't let me set foot on Parkum until he'd told me about you. He warned me not to be a nuisance.'

'You mean Halberstaedt,' he corrected her. 'The mayor.'

'The second most important person on the island – besides yourself. He didn't hesitate to inform me of that as well. I'll be sure to follow his advice and park my delectable bottom somewhere else, but first you're going to give me a chance to explain.'

'Delectable bottom? Did he really say that?'

'Yes. In any case, I don't intend to go anywhere until you've heard me out. I'm only asking for five minutes and then you can tell me to my face.'

'Tell you what?'

'Whether or not you're interested in my case.'

'I don't have time for patients,' he said weakly. 'Please, just go.'

'I will go, I promise, but I want you to hear my story. It'll only take five minutes, and you won't regret a single second.'

Viktor hesitated. His curiosity was getting the better of him and besides, he would never be able to focus on his work. He felt too weary to continue the debate.

'Come on, Dr Larenz, I won't bite.' She smiled at him.

The parquet floor groaned as she took another step towards him. Now he could smell her perfume. *Opium.*

'Five minutes?'

'I promise.'

He shrugged. Given the situation, five minutes were neither here nor there. If he threw her out now, she would probably wait outside the house, pacing up and down and distracting him from his thoughts.

'All right then.' He made a point of looking at his watch. 'Five minutes and then we're done.'

# 4

Viktor went to the mantelpiece above the fireplace where an antique Meissen teapot was resting on a trivet. Realizing that the woman was watching him closely, he pulled himself together and made an effort to be polite.

'Can I offer you some tea? I was about to make a pot.'

The woman smiled and shook her head. 'Thank you, but no. My five minutes would be over before I could drink it.'

'As you wish. But at least sit down and take off your coat.'

He picked up a stack of old newspapers from the leather armchair that went with the couch. Decades ago, his father had configured the three-piece suite so that everyone, when seated, had a view of the sea and the hearth. The sitting room was the perfect place to curl up with a book.

Viktor returned to his desk and made himself comfortable. His beautiful young guest sat down but seemed disinclined to remove her cashmere coat.

In the short silence that followed, a huge wave crashed against the beach. The water rushed back into the sea, foaming and seething.

Viktor glanced at his watch again.

'Very well, Miss ... I'm sorry, I didn't catch your name.'

'Anna. My name is Anna Glass. I'm a novelist.'

'A famous one?'

'Not unless you're interested in children's books. Most of my readers are aged six to thirteen. Do you have children?'

'Yes, I mean, no. I . . .' The words came forcefully and abruptly, driven by a sudden rush of pain. He realized that she was checking the mantelpiece for photos. *Surely she must have seen the headlines?* He changed the subject to avoid further questions.

'Which part of Germany are you from? I can't detect an accent.'

'Berlin. I was born there. But I sell more copies overseas. Japan was my best market, but it's all in the past.'

'In the past?'

'I haven't finished a book for years.'

The conversation had lapsed into the standard pattern of questions and answers characterizing the patient–therapist dynamic. Viktor was back to being the psychiatrist again.

'When was your last book published?'

'Five years ago. After that, I started another project – a children's book, of course. I thought it was going to be my best. It almost seemed to write itself, but I never got past the first couple of chapters.'

'Why was that?'

'Health problems. It happened very suddenly. I had to go to hospital.'

'What was wrong with you?'

'To be honest, I don't think anyone really knows. They seemed pretty baffled at the Park.'

'The Park? Not the Park Clinic in Dahlem?'

Viktor was unable to hide his astonishment. The information put a whole new spin on the conversation. For one thing, it meant that Ms Glass was very wealthy. Only a bestselling author would be able to afford private treatment at the Park. It also meant that her problems were of a serious nature. Unlike the majority of famous clinics, the Park didn't cater to celebrities with drug and alcohol addictions. The Park only dealt with acute psychological disorders. In the glory days of his career, he had been asked to advise on some of the more problematic cases and he could testify to the professionalism of the place. With some of the country's leading experts at its disposal, the Park was at the forefront of therapeutic advances and had chalked up some notable successes. All the same, he had never seen a patient make such a complete recovery as the young woman sitting opposite him. She seemed perfectly lucid and alert.

'How long were you there?'

'Forty-seven months in total.'

Viktor was lost for words. Forty-seven months? She was either a consummate liar or seriously disturbed. *She's probably both*, he decided.

'I was locked in a room and stuffed with pills for nearly four years. I barely knew who I was, let alone what was happening.'

'And the diagnosis?'

'Haven't you guessed by now, Dr Larenz? They said I was schizophrenic. It's why I came to you.'

Viktor leant back thoughtfully and considered her words. Schizophrenia was his specialism. Or at least it had been.

'How did you come to be admitted?'

'I called Professor Malzius.'

'You called the director and requested to be admitted?'

'It seemed like a good idea. Everyone speaks highly of the Park, and I didn't know where to turn. I would have come to you if I'd known.'

'Who referred you to me?'

'A consultant at the Park. I was living in such a fug that I had no idea what was best for me. He stopped my meds and told me to go to you.'

'What were they giving you?'

'Pretty much everything. Truxal and fluspirilene, but mainly flupentixol.'

Truxal, fluspirilene and flupentixol were standard antipsychotic drugs. The clinicians at the Park knew what they were doing.

'And none of them helped?'

'The symptoms got worse. Even after I stopped taking the medication, it took weeks to find my feet. In my opinion, that's proof enough that drugs aren't the solution to my particular condition.'

'What's different about your condition?'

'I'm a novelist.'

'So you said.'

'It's probably best if I give you an example.' Her eyes, which until now had been fixed on him unwaveringly, shifted to an imaginary object in the distance. During his years in practice, Viktor had opted for face-to-face discussions instead of the traditional analyst's couch. Ms Glass's behaviour was nothing out of the ordinary. Patients tended to avoid his gaze whenever they were endeavouring to give an accurate account of an important and traumatic event. Or when they were lying.

'The first thing I ever wrote was a short story for a competition. I was thirteen years old at the time. The competition was open to secondary school pupils throughout Berlin and the subject was "The Meaning of Life". My story was about a group of young people who set up a scientific experiment. I submitted the manuscript, and that's when the problems started.'

'What kind of problems?'

'I was at a party at the Four Seasons hotel in Grunewald. My best friend had just turned fourteen and her parents had hired out the ballroom. I slipped out to the toilet and saw her in the lobby. She was waiting at reception.'

'Your best friend?'

'No, Julia.'

'Julia who?'

'Julia. A character in my story. I introduced her in the opening paragraph.'

'Let's get this straight: the woman in the lobby *resembled* a character in your story?'

'No.' Ms Glass shook her head firmly. 'She didn't look like Julia; she *was* Julia.'

'What makes you think that?'

'Because she repeated word-for-word the first line of the story.'

'Pardon?'

She lowered her voice and looked Viktor in the eye. 'Julia leant over the counter and said to the man at reception: "Listen honey, I'm going to do something special. How about you fix me up with a room?"'

Viktor met her searching gaze. 'Didn't it occur to you that it might be a coincidence?'

'Sure. I gave it an awful lot of thought. But it seemed too much of a coincidence, given what happened next.'

'Namely?'

'Julia did exactly as I described. She stuck a pistol in her mouth and blew her brains out.'

Viktor stared at her, aghast.

'You're not . . .'

'Serious? I'm afraid so. Julia was the beginning of a nightmare that has been haunting me for nearly twenty years. Some phases are more intense than others. But I'm a writer, Dr Larenz. It's my curse.'

Viktor knew exactly what was coming next; he could have predicted every single word.

'My characters come alive. I only have to imagine a person, and I see them, hear them and sometimes even speak to them. I create them, and they walk into my life. Call it schizophrenia if you will, but that's the nature of my condition, my own particular mental tick.'

She leant towards him. 'And there you have it. I decided to come to you.'

Viktor looked at her and refrained from saying anything. There were too many conflicting thoughts, too many emotions.

'Well, Dr Larenz?'

'Well, what?'

'Are you interested in my case? I've come all this way to ask you to treat me. Say you'll agree.'

Viktor checked his watch. The five minutes were over.

# 5

Looking back, Viktor decided that the signs were there from the beginning. Had he listened more carefully, he might have realized that something was wrong. Very wrong. But no amount of insight could have averted the disaster. It would only have brought things to a head.

The fact was, Anna Glass had outmanoeuvred him. She had forced her way into his home and knocked him off guard. Her case was unusual; so unusual that for five carefree minutes he had forgotten about himself and his problems. He was glad of the respite, but his decision still stood: he had no desire to be her therapist. After a short but firm exchange, he convinced her to return to the mainland on the early morning ferry and make an appointment with Professor van Druisen.

'I have my reasons,' he said curtly when she demanded to know why. 'For one thing, I haven't practised in over four years.'

'I'm sure you'd still know how to treat me.'

'It's not a question of knowledge; I just . . .'

'You don't *want* to treat me.'

*Exactly*, he thought. Something warned him against telling his visitor about Josy. If no one at the clinic had told her of the tragedy, he had no intention of volunteering the information himself.

'In a case of your complexity, it would be irresponsible and unprofessional to offer analysis without researching your condition first. Especially without the facilities that a proper clinic would offer.'

'Researching my condition? Dr Larenz, you're an expert! What's the first question you would have asked if I were in your practice in Berlin?'

Viktor smiled at her clumsy attempt to waylay him. 'I would have asked you when the hallucinations first started, but I . . .'

'The episode in the hotel wasn't the first time,' she broke in quickly. 'It started much earlier than that. But I never experienced anything so . . .' She paused for a moment, considering her words. 'So *realistic*. So convincing. My previous hallucinations were vaguer and less tangible, but Julia was real. I saw her, I heard the gun go off, and the next moment, her brains were all over the lobby. She was the first character from one of my stories to come alive. Of course, like most schizophrenics, I had a history of mental illness.'

'Such as?' Viktor decided to give the woman another five minutes before he escorted her to the door.

'It's hard to know where to begin. I'd say the symptoms started when I was a child.'

He waited for her to continue and took a sip of his rapidly cooling Assam tea. It tasted bitter.

'My father was a GI. He fought for the Allies and stayed in Berlin. He was a DJ on the American Forces Network for a while. Women loved him and he was a bit of a local hero. Anyway, he had a string of blonde dalliances in the back room of the military casino, and one of his many girlfriends fell pregnant. Her name was Laura, she was a Berliner, and the baby was me.'

'I see. I notice you mentioned your father first?'

'He died when I was eight. Professor Malzius says the accident was the first traumatic event of my childhood.'

'What accident?'

'My father died in a military hospital. It was a straightforward appendicectomy, but he developed a clot. He hadn't been given compression stockings. The thrombosis was fatal.'

'How dreadful,' said Viktor with feeling. He was always appalled by the damage caused by incompetent doctors. Their carelessness brought terrible suffering on patients and their families.

'How did you cope with your father's death?'

'Badly. We lived in an end-of-terrace house near Andrew Barracks in the American sector. We adopted a mongrel, a stray called Terry, who lived in our backyard. My father couldn't stand him and banned him from the house. Most of the time he was tied up on a lead by the door. I remember Mum telling me that the operation had gone wrong. As soon as she left the house, I fetched one of Dad's baseball bats – a heavy one made of metal

SEBASTIAN FITZEK

– and went into the yard. Terry's lead was so short that he could hardly move, let alone run away. His legs buckled as soon as I hit him. I could see him whimpering and grovelling on the ground, but I didn't stop. I kept hitting him and hitting him. I was only eight years old and out of my mind with fury and hurt. After about ten blows, I must have snapped his spine. He lay there, howling in agony and coughing up blood, and I battered him to a pulp. He didn't even look like a dog when I was finished.'

Viktor tried not to show his disgust. 'What made you do it?' he asked calmly.

'I loved my father more than anyone in the world. Terry came next. For some reason I got it into my head that I didn't want Terry if I couldn't have my dad. I was punishing him for being alive.'

'It must have been very stressful.'

'It was. But not for the reason you think.'

'I beg your pardon?'

'The story doesn't end there. I'd lost my father and beaten an innocent dog to death, but that wasn't what really upset me.'

'No?'

'What upset me was that Terry didn't exist. I made him up. We adopted a cat, but never a dog. I still have nightmares about what I did to Terry, but I know for a fact that it was a delusion, a product of my illness.'

'When did you find out it wasn't real?'

'Much later. I started seeing a therapist when I was

about eighteen and after a while the truth came out. It was the first time I summoned the courage to mention it to anyone. I didn't want people knowing that I'd murdered my dog. They'd only think I was crazy.'

*The poor girl*, thought Viktor, giving Sindbad an absent-minded pat. The retriever was sleeping peacefully at his feet, untroubled by the distressing revelations. Anna had suffered dreadfully because of an act of cruelty that she had never committed. That was the tyranny of schizophrenia. Most delusions had the effect of making the sufferer feel useless, evil and unworthy of existence. It wasn't uncommon for patients to surrender to their imaginary taskmasters and take their own lives. Viktor took another look at his watch and was astonished to see how late it was. He would have to leave the *Bunte* interview for another day.

'Very good, Ms Glass.'

He stood up purposefully to signal that it was time for her to go. He took a step towards Anna and felt surprisingly light-headed.

'I hope I've made it sufficiently clear that I'm not in a position to treat you,' he said firmly. He wanted to escort her to the door but he was afraid he might sway.

Anna looked at him impassively and rose to her feet.

'I understand,' she said, unexpectedly brightly. 'Thanks for listening. I'll be sure to follow your advice.'

Viktor watched her walk to the door and was reminded of something. He tried to pin down the memory, but it eluded him.

Anna turned round. 'Are you feeling all right, Dr Larenz?'

'I'm fine, thank you,' he replied, embarrassed that she had noticed his dizziness.

The truth was, he felt as if he were recovering from a long voyage at sea.

'Where are you staying?' he enquired, trying to move the conversation on. He opened the front door and Anna stepped on to the porch.

'At the Anchor.'

He nodded. *Of course*. The Anchor was the only guesthouse that stayed open throughout the winter months. It was run by Trudi, whose husband had drowned on a fishing expedition three years earlier. She never turned anyone away.

'Are you sure you're all right?' she persisted.

'Absolutely. I get a bit dizzy when I stand up too quickly.' He hoped that he wasn't succumbing to the flu.

She seemed satisfied with his answer. 'I'd better get going. I need to pack my things and get an early night. I don't want to miss the first ferry.'

Viktor was pleased to hear it. The sooner she left Parkum, the better. He wanted to be left alone.

He shook hands with her again and they parted on affable, almost friendly, terms.

Later, Viktor wished that he had listened more attentively and noticed the warning signs. But that was the trouble with hindsight. At the time, it didn't occur to him to check that she was really gone. She must have counted on his trusting nature. As soon as the door was closed, she made no secret of her true intentions and set off on a northerly bearing – in the opposite direction to the Anchor.

# 6

No sooner had he got rid of Anna, than he was disturbed again. There was another knock at the door. This time it was Halberstaedt, the mayor.

'You did a great job with the generator,' said Viktor, shaking the old man's hand. 'The house was warm when I arrived.'

'My pleasure, Dr Larenz,' said Halberstaedt gruffly, snatching back his hand.

'So what brings you all this way in such blustery weather? The mail run isn't for another couple of days, is it?'

'I'm not here about the mail run.'

Halberstaedt was clutching a piece of driftwood in his left hand. He thwacked it against the soles of his black wellingtons to dislodge the sand from the grooves.

'I see. Would you like to come in? There's rain on the way.'

'Thanks, but I don't want to keep you. I was just wondering . . .'

'Yes?'

'The woman who was here just now. Who is she?'

Viktor was taken aback by his bluntness. It was unlike the reserved and courteous Halberstaedt to pry.

'Tell me to mind my own business, but I'd advise you to be careful,' continued the mayor, pausing to spit out his chewing tobacco which flew over the side of the veranda and landed in the sand. 'Very careful indeed.'

Narrowing his eyes, Viktor squinted at him disapprovingly. He didn't like the advice or the tone in which it was given.

'What exactly are you implying?'

'I don't beat about the bush, Dr Larenz. There's something funny about that woman. She's not right in the head.'

It was natural for people to be suspicious of mental illness, but Viktor was surprised that Halberstaedt had picked up so quickly on Anna's fragile state of mind. He wondered what the mayor thought of him. *God knows I'm fragile too ...*

'There's no need to worry about Ms—'

'It's not *her* I'm worried about. It's you,' said Halberstaedt sharply.

The hiatus was over. Anna's sudden appearance and her horrifying story had distracted him for a while, but now the thoughts were back. A million different triggers could conjure the image of Josy in his mind. Raised voices were among them.

'What do you mean?'

'What I said. You need to be careful. I've been living on this island for forty-two years and I've seen people come and go. Some were good, decent folks like you who never made any trouble. Others weren't so welcome. I know a bad egg when I see one; I've got an instinct for it. I knew as soon as I saw her that she was up to no good.'

'Do you have any evidence? Did she say something to alarm you?'

'I never talked to her. I saw her get off the ferry, and I followed her here.'

*That's funny*, thought Viktor, remembering Anna's version of the story. There was no reason for her to lie.

'She dropped by the hardware store a couple of hours ago. Hinnerk said that she was acting very strangely.'

'Could you be more specific?'

'She asked for a weapon.'

'A weapon?'

'She made him show her a harpoon and a flare gun, but she bought a carving knife and some fishing twine instead. Why would she do that?'

'No idea,' said Viktor, who didn't know what to make of the story. Parkum was a sleepy little place. What would Ms Glass want with a weapon?

'Right you are.' Halberstaedt pulled the black hood of his parka over his head. 'I'd best be off. Sorry for bothering you.'

'Not at all; it was kind of you to come.'

Halberstaedt descended the steps to the path and walked to the low gate. He stopped at the picket fence and turned round.

'One last thing, Doctor. We were all very sorry to hear the news.'

Viktor nodded. There was no need for Halberstaedt to be more specific. People had been offering Viktor their condolences for four years.

'I thought we might help you,' said the mayor.

'What do you mean?'

'As soon as you got off the ferry, I said to myself that a change of scene would do you good. I thought you were going to put the past behind you and get some colour in your cheeks. The trouble is . . .'

'What?'

'You look paler than ever. Is something the matter?'

*I'm trapped in a nightmare*, thought Viktor, *the nightmare of my life. And you're not making it any easier.* He kept his thoughts to himself, shook his head firmly and almost lost his balance. He was feeling dizzy again.

Halberstaedt closed the gate behind him and looked at him sternly. 'Suit yourself. Maybe it's nothing, maybe it's not. Either way, remember what I said about that woman.'

Viktor merely nodded.

'Look after yourself, Doctor. Keep an eye out over the next few days. I've got a bad feeling about this.'

'I'll be careful. Thanks for the concern.'

Viktor locked the front door and peered after Halberstaedt through the spyhole. The perspective was rather limited, and within seconds the mayor was out of sight.

*What was all that about?* he wondered.

Eventually he would discover the truth – but by then it would be too late.

# 7

*Four days before the truth, Parkum*

> *Bunte: Do you still live in hope?*

The second question was the worst. After a bad night's sleep and an uninspired breakfast, it was ten o'clock by the time that Viktor started work. Thirty minutes later, he was still staring at a blank screen. At least there was a reason for his sluggishness. He was almost certainly developing the flu. Yesterday's dizziness seemed to have cured itself, but he had a sore throat and a runny nose. All the same, he wanted to make some headway with the interview.

> *Hope.*

It was tempting to answer with a question of his own:

> *Hope for what? That Josy is still alive or that someone will find her corpse?*

A strong gust shook the lattice window. Viktor vaguely recollected hearing a weather warning on the news. Since yesterday, the island had been bracing itself for the arrival of Hurricane Anton, the tail end of which was set to hit Parkum that afternoon. A grey bank of rain was stacking up over the sea and the first showers, pushed landwards by the ferocious wind, had started to lash the coast. The temperature had fallen sharply overnight and, thanks to the feeble output of the diesel generator, it was chilly enough for the fire to be useful as well as pretty. In fact, it was so dismal outside that even the fishing boats and ferries were heeding the coastguard's advice. From his desk by the window, Viktor was unable to make out a single vessel on the angry-looking sea. He shifted his gaze to the screen.

*Hope.*

Viktor clenched his fists and spread his fingers over the keyboard without touching the keys. On first reading, the question had blasted through his brain, breaking down an invisible dam and flushing out his mind. After the initial emptiness, a single thought took shape, a memory of his father's last days. At seventy-four years of age, Gustav Larenz had been diagnosed with a lymphoma. The cancer caused him constant and excruciating pain, for which he was given a steady stream of morphine, but in the final stages of his illness, no drug in the world was strong enough to take away his suffering. He was tortured by pounding migraines whose potency was reduced to a tolerable level every couple of hours by a fresh dose of pills. Viktor remembered how he had described it: 'It's like living under a bell jar, surrounded by fog.'

Now, years later, he understood. His hope was hidden under a bell jar. He wondered whether the father's symptoms had been visited on the son, passed from one generation to the next like a hereditary disease. *Only the cancer isn't attacking my lymph glands; it's invading my mind, eroding my spirit.*

Viktor took a deep breath and began to type.

Yes, he lived in hope. He lived in hope that his housekeeper would announce the arrival of a visitor who would wait in the hallway, cap in hand, and decline the invitation to join him in the lounge. He lived in hope that the uniformed stranger would look him in the eye and say nothing for a moment. And at that point he would know. He would know long before the officer opened his mouth to utter the most final of phrases: 'I'm sorry for your loss.'

That was Viktor's hope.

Isabell hoped for the opposite. He had no idea where she got the strength, but he could tell that her prayers were the reverse of his. Deep down she believed in the future. She believed in a future in which she would come back from a morning's horse riding and see Josy's bicycle in the drive. And before she could pick it up and put it in the shed, Josy would come storming down the path from the lake, laughing and dragging her father by the hand.

From a distance, the happy, healthy and excitable little girl would shout out, 'What's for lunch, Mummy?' and things would return to normal. Isabell would take it in her stride. She wouldn't be surprised and she wouldn't ask questions. She would run her hand over Josy's blonde hair, which would be a couple of inches longer than usual, and accept that she was back and that the family was reunited. She would welcome her return with the same acceptance that she had shown day after day for nearly four years. That was Isabell's unspoken hope.

*Does that answer your question?*

Viktor realized with detachment that he was talking out loud. This time Ida von Strachwitz, the journalist from *Bunte*, was his imaginary listener. He was supposed to email her with the answers in two days' time.

Viktor's laptop made a noise that reminded him of an ancient coffee machine spitting the last drops of water into the filter. He decided to delete the last few lines. To his surprise, he discovered that there was nothing to delete. The sum of thirty minutes' work was a single sentence, which had no obvious connection to the question.

> *The gulf between not knowing and knowing*
> *Is the difference between life and death.*

There was no time for Viktor to expand on what he had written because a moment later the telephone rang. No one had called the house since his arrival. The shrill ring and raucous echo shattered the tranquillity of the beach house and made him jump. He let it ring four times before he picked up the heavy receiver of the black dial phone. Like most things in the house, the old-fashioned machine had belonged to his father. It was positioned on a low table next to the bookcase.

'I hope I'm not disturbing you.'

Viktor suppressed a groan. He had been half-expecting her to call. At the sound of her voice, the dizziness returned along with the sore throat and other symptoms of his cold.

'I thought we reached an agreement, Ms Glass?'

'Sorry,' said a small voice in reply.

'Aren't you supposed to be leaving this morning? What time is your ferry?'

'That's why I called. I can't go.'

'Can't go?' Viktor looked to the ceiling in irritation and noticed a few cobwebs in the corner. 'Listen, Ms Glass, we went over this yesterday. You're in remission at the moment and you're well enough to catch a ferry. I want you to go to Berlin and make an appointment with Professor van Druisen. I'm afraid I—'

'I can't,' said Anna quietly. Viktor guessed the reason before she had time to explain.

'It's the ferry. Today's sailings have been cancelled because of the storm. I'm stuck.'

# 8

He sensed it as soon as he hung up the call. There had been something in her voice. It gave him the impression that she had arranged the storm with the express intention of interrupting his work and sabotaging his efforts to lay the past to rest. She had sounded as if she had something to tell him, something so important that she had gone to the trouble and expense of coming all the way from Berlin – and yet she had omitted to mention it yesterday for reasons best known to herself. She hadn't said what it was, but he knew with absolute certainty that she was prepared to stay on the island until she got it off her chest. Fearing that she would arrive at any moment, he decided to have a shower and get dressed. In the bathroom, he dissolved a couple of aspirin in some water and gulped them down on an empty stomach. He could feel the pressure building behind his eyes, a sure sign that a migraine was on its way. Under normal circumstances he would have taken a couple of painkillers at the first hint of trouble, but flupirtine made him sleepy, and he wanted to have his wits about him when his unwelcome visitor arrived.

As a result, he felt bunged up but not drowsy when a

growling Sindbad alerted him to Anna's arrival. It was early afternoon.

'I was out for a stroll and I saw the light in the parlour,' she said brightly when he opened the door.

Viktor frowned. Out for a stroll? Only the most dedicated dog owners would venture out in weather like this. It wasn't raining heavily, but the perpetual drizzle was miserable enough. And Anna, in her expensive cashmere suit and high-heeled shoes, was hardly dressed for the conditions. The walk from the village took at least fifteen minutes and the potholed track was flooded already. But Anna's pumps looked as pristine and elegant as ever. And, in spite of the absence of umbrella and headscarf, her hair was perfectly dry.

'Dr Larenz? Is this a bad time?'

Viktor realized that he had been staring at her mistrustfully.

'Yes, I mean, no, I . . .' he stuttered. 'Forgive me. I wasn't expecting visitors and I've come down with a bit of a cold.'

He remembered what Halberstaedt had told him. It made him doubly reluctant to invite her in.

'Oh.' Anna's face fell. 'I'm sorry to hear it.'

Out to sea, a flash of lightning streaked across the sky, bathing the cottage in sudden light. It was followed by a low roll of thunder. The storm was getting closer. Irritated, Viktor realized that he could hardly close the door on his troublesome guest. Good manners dictated that he put up with her company, at least until the worst of the weather was over.

'Since you've taken the trouble to drop by, I suppose you'd better come in for some tea,' he said reluctantly. Anna jumped at the offer. She was smiling again and Viktor thought he glimpsed a look of triumph on her face. She reminded him of a small child whose pestering had been rewarded with a bag of sweets.

She followed him into the sitting room where they resumed their positions of the previous day; Anna, legs crossed elegantly, on the couch and Viktor with his back to the window by the desk.

'Help yourself to tea.'

He raised his cup and nodded towards the teapot that was sitting on the mantelpiece over a tea light.

'Thank you – maybe later.'

Viktor's sore throat was markedly worse. He took a large gulp of Assam tea. The bitter taste was more pronounced than last time.

'Are you feeling all right, Dr Larenz?'

She had asked him the same question yesterday. It bothered him that she seemed to see straight through him. He was the psychiatrist, after all.

'I'm fine, thanks.'

'You haven't smiled since I got here. I hope I haven't done anything to incur your displeasure. I had every intention of catching the ferry, believe me. I wasn't to know that the service would be suspended.'

'Did they tell you when the boat will be back in action?'

'They said forty-eight hours. Twenty-four at a push.'

*Knowing my luck, she'll be here for a week*, thought Viktor, who remembered being stranded on Parkum with his father for at least that long.

'Maybe you could give me another consultation, seeing as I'm here,' she suggested boldly, smiling her gentle smile.

*She wants to get something off her chest.*

'Another consultation? Ms Glass, I'm not your therapist. Yesterday was an informal chat, nothing more. A patch of bad weather won't change my mind.'

'Fine, then let's keep talking. Yesterday's chat really helped.'

*She wants to tell me something and she won't stop bothering me until I hear her out.*

Viktor held her gaze for a few seconds and gave in when he realized that she was determined not to look away.

'All right, I suppose we can chat . . .'

*Let's finish whatever it is that you've started*, he added to himself.

Anna leant back happily on the couch and proceeded to tell Viktor the most appalling story of his life.

# 9

'What are you working on at the moment?' he asked to get the ball rolling.

He had woken up that morning with a question on his mind. *Who will she bring to life next?*

'I don't write fiction anymore. Or at least, not what most people would understand by fiction.'

'How would you describe it?'

'These days I only write about myself, so *autobiography*, I suppose. It kills three birds with one stone: it allows me to indulge my literary bent, it gives me a way of coming to terms with my past, and it rules out the possibility of fictional characters coming alive and driving me crazy.'

'I see. Then tell me about your most recent breakdown – the one that culminated in your admission to the Park.'

Anna took a deep breath and folded her hands as if in prayer.

'Very well. The last character who came to life was the heroine of a children's book. A modern fairy tale.'

'Can you tell me about the plot?'

'It centred on a little girl called Charlotte. A delicate

slip of a thing with angelic blonde hair – the sort you see on commercials for biscuits and chocolate. You know the type.'

'As hallucinations go, I can think of worse.'

'True. Charlotte was a darling. People found her adorable. Her father was the king and they lived in a palace on an island.'

'How did the story start?'

'With a quest. One day Charlotte fell ill – seriously ill.'

Viktor, who had been preparing to take another sip of tea, replaced his cup on the desk. Anna had his full attention.

'She lost weight, became frail and sickly, and was struck down by all kinds of mysterious infections. One by one, the king consulted every doctor in the kingdom, but no one knew what was wrong with his daughter. It wasn't long before the royal couple were frantic with worry. Meanwhile, poor Charlotte was declining by the day.'

Viktor was so absorbed that he forgot to breathe.

'One day she decided to take charge of her own destiny. She ran away from home.'

*Josy.*

In spite of his best efforts, Viktor caught himself thinking about his daughter.

'I beg your pardon?' said Anna, puzzled.

Viktor ran a hand nervously through his hair. He

must have spoken out loud. 'Nothing. I didn't mean to interrupt. Carry on.'

'So Charlotte set off on a quest to find the cause of her illness. I suppose you could call it a parable. A little girl refuses to give up hope and sets off into the big wide world on her own.'

*No*, thought Viktor. *This can't be happening.* His mind ground slowly to a halt. It was the same feeling of paralysis that he had experienced in Dr Grohlke's clinic; the same catatonic numbness that had accompanied him every single day of his life until he had decided to call off the search for Josy.

'Are you sure you're all right, Dr Larenz?'

'Pardon? Oh, sorry . . .' He stared at the fingers of his right hand which were drumming nervously on the antique mahogany desk.

'Forgive me, I should stop drinking so much tea. But tell me more about Charlotte. How does the story end? What happened to her?'

*Where did Josy go?*

'I don't know.'

'Surely you know how your own story ends?' he asked roughly. The question sounded more aggressive than he had intended, but Anna seemed unperturbed.

'I told you before, Dr Larenz, I never got past the first few chapters. And that's why Charlotte came after me. It's how the nightmare started.'

*Nightmare?*

'What do you mean?'

'Charlotte was the last of my characters to come alive. What we experienced together was so stressful that I broke down completely. That's when I was admitted to the Park.'

'Let's back up a little. Tell me exactly what happened.'

Viktor knew he was breaking the rules. It was too early for the patient to discuss the trauma, but he simply had to know. Anna bowed her head and stared at the ground. He persisted, but this time more gently.

'When did you first see Charlotte?'

'About four years ago in Berlin. It was winter.'

*November 26*, thought Viktor.

'I was on my way to the shops when I heard an awful noise: screeching tyres, the crunch of metal on metal, splintering glass. It sounded like a car accident. I can remember thinking "I hope no one's hurt", then I turned round to see a girl in the middle of the road. She was rooted to the spot. The crash was obviously her fault.'

Viktor sat rigid in his chair.

'Suddenly, as if she could sense I was there, she turned round and smiled at me. I recognized her right away. It was Charlotte – the little girl from my book. She ran over and took me by the hand.'

*Such frail, thin arms. So delicate.*

'My mind seemed to shut down. On the one hand, I knew Charlotte wasn't real; she had to be a delusion. On the other, she was standing right beside me. In the end, I had to believe the evidence of my eyes. So I followed her.'

'Followed her? Which way? Where did she go?'

'Why? Does it make a difference?' asked Anna, blinking in confusion. She seemed put out.

'Not in the slightest. I'm sorry, go on.'

Anna cleared her throat and stood up. 'If you don't mind, Dr Larenz, I'd like to take a break. I know I pressured you into this conversation, but I thought I was ready, and I'm not. The hallucinations were extremely traumatic. It's not easy for me to discuss them.'

'I understand,' said Viktor, managing to sound sympathetic even though he was desperate for her to carry on. He got to his feet as well.

'You won't have to worry about me bothering you again. With any luck, the ferry will be up and running tomorrow.'

*No!*

Viktor tried feverishly to think of a reason for making her stay. He couldn't allow her to leave the island, although that was exactly what he had made her promise to do.

He hovered awkwardly in the middle of the room. 'One last question: what was the book called?'

'I hadn't decided. I only had a working title: *Nine.*'

'*Nine?*'

'Charlotte was nine years old when she ran away from home.'

'Oh.'

*Younger than Josy.*

Viktor was surprised at himself. He had come very close to believing Anna's story. In fact, he had almost hoped that her delusions were somehow connected to the truth.

He took a few steps towards her and realized that his symptoms were getting worse. The aspirin had done nothing to get rid of his migraine, his temples were still throbbing, and his eyes were watering. Anna was standing in front of him, but her contours were blurred, as if he were seeing her through a glass of water. He blinked, his vision cleared a little, and when he looked again, he saw an expression on her face that he couldn't quite decipher. Then it came to him: he and Anna had met before. He knew her from a long time ago, but he couldn't put his finger on when or how. It was like recognizing an actress but not knowing which characters she played or what she was called in real life.

He helped her clumsily into her coat and escorted her to the door. Anna stepped outside, then turned round suddenly. Her mouth was almost touching his face.

'Oh, that reminds me. You know you asked about the title?'

'Yes?' Viktor took a step backwards, feeling a rush of nervous energy.

'I don't suppose it's relevant, but the book had a subtitle. Oddly enough, it didn't have anything to do with the plot. The idea came to me in the bath and I went along with it because it sounded sort of funny.'

'What was it?'

For a split second he wondered whether he really wanted to know. Then it was too late.

'*The Blue Cat*,' said Anna. 'Don't ask me why. I was going to have a picture of a blue cat on the jacket.'

# 10

'OK, let's get this straight . . .'

Viktor could tell that the paunchy detective was shaking his head incredulously on the other end of the line. He had rung the PI as soon as Anna left the house.

'You're telling me that a mental patient turned up on your doorstep in Parkum?'

'Correct.'

'And this woman is convinced that she's being hounded by characters from her own books.'

'Yes.'

'And you want me to find out whether the delusional ramblings of Ms . . . What was her name again?'

'Sorry, Kai, but I'd rather not say. She's a patient – not *my* patient – but a patient all the same. Everything she tells me is confidential.'

*To a point.*

'And you reckon Ms What's-Her-Name's hallucinations are connected to Josy's disappearance?'

'Right.'

'You know what I think?'

'You think I'm crazy.'

'That's putting it mildly.'

'I don't blame you, Kai. But I can't dismiss what she told me. It's too much of a coincidence.'

'You can't – or you don't want to?'

Viktor pretended not to hear. 'A small girl succumbs to a mysterious illness and disappears without trace. And not just anywhere – *in Berlin*.'

'OK,' said Kai, 'but the woman could have been lying when she said she hadn't read the papers. What if she knew about Josy?'

'I considered that too, but Josy's health problems weren't public knowledge.'

Viktor remembered how the police had advised them to keep back the information regarding Josy's sickness. The media would have seized on the story of the mystery symptoms and sensationalized the case.

Besides, there was another advantage to withholding the details, as the young officer in charge of the investigation explained, 'It gives us a means of identifying the real abductor. We're expecting all kinds of calls from opportunists who claim to be holding Josy in the hope of getting their hands on your cash.'

The tactic proved effective. The appeals for information about Josy prompted a flurry of calls from people all claiming to be the kidnapper. In response to the question 'How is Josephine?' they invariably reported that she was doing 'just fine' or 'quite well, considering the circumstances'. Both replies were definitively wrong. Josephine fainted on a daily basis and being abducted was hardly likely to have improved her health.

'OK, Doc, so a little girl gets sick and runs away from home,' said the PI. 'So far, so good, but what about that stuff about a royal palace and an island?'

'Technically, Schwanenwerder *is* an island. It's only accessible from Berlin-Zehlendorf by a bridge. And the house is practically a palace, you said so yourself. As for the stuff about the princess, Isabell used to call ... or rather, Isabell calls our daughter her *little princess*. It all adds up.'

'Listen, Victor, don't get me wrong. We've known each other for four years now, and I'd like to think we're friends – but you shouldn't take this woman seriously. She hasn't told you anything you didn't already know. Her story's like a horoscope – too vague to be useful.'

'You're probably right, but I owe it to Josy to check out every possible lead, no matter how unlikely.'

'All right, you're the boss. But let's remind ourselves of the facts. The last credible sighting of Josephine came from an elderly couple who saw a man walk out of Dr Grohlke's clinic with a little girl. They didn't challenge the guy because they assumed he was the father. Their statement was backed up by the man who runs the kiosk on the corner. Your daughter was abducted by a middle-aged man. And she was twelve years old, not nine.'

'Don't forget the blue cat! Josy's favourite toy was a fluffy blue cat called Nepomuk.'

'Hallelujah! Supposing this woman abducted your daughter, why would she come to you? She hides out with Josy for four years and then one day, out of the blue, she hops on a ferry to Parkum. It doesn't make sense.'

'I'm not saying she was responsible for Josy's disappearance; I'm saying she knows something, that's all. And I'll do my utmost to get it out of her in the course of her analysis.'

'You're seeing her again?'

'I invited her for another chat tomorrow morning. I hope she'll come; I was a bit unfriendly at first.'

'Why don't you cut to the chase and ask what she knows about Josy?'

'How?'

'Show her a picture. Ask if she recognizes her, and if she says yes, call the police.'

'I've only got a photocopy of a newspaper article. I didn't bring any decent photos.'

'I can fax you one.'

'It's not worth it. I wouldn't be able to use it – yet.'

'Why not?'

'In one respect my patient was definitely telling the truth: she's schizophrenic. As a therapist, I have to earn her trust. She's already signalled to me that she doesn't want to talk about what happened. If she thinks that I'm accusing her of perpetrating a crime, she'll never speak to me again. She'll shut down completely. I can't take that risk if there's the slightest chance that Josy might be alive. She's my last hope.'

*Hope.*

'You know what, Viktor? Hope is like a shard of glass.

Tread on it, and you'll end up wincing with every step. The best policy is to tweezer it out. Sure, it will hurt like billy-o and the wound will take a while to heal, but after that you can walk again. There's a thing called grieving, and you should try it. The kid's been missing for four years! For Christ's sake, Viktor, a jumbled story from a mental patient isn't exactly a promising lead!'

Unknown to the PI, his perorations on the nature of hope had furnished Viktor with the answer to *Bunte*'s second question.

'OK, Kai, we'll make a deal. I'll stop searching for Josy in return for one last favour.'

'What?'

'Find out if there's any record of a car accident taking place in the vicinity of Grohlke's clinic between 15.30 and 16.15 on November 26. Can you do that for me?'

'Yep. But in the meantime I want you to back off and put all your energy into finishing your bloody interview. Understood?'

Viktor simply thanked him for his help. It seemed silly to make promises that he had no intention of keeping.

# 11

## *Three days before the truth, Parkum*

*Bunte: It was obviously an immensely stressful time for you. What helped you cope?*

Viktor chuckled. In a few moments, his next session with Anna would begin, provided she turned up. They had made the arrangement the previous day, but Anna had refused to commit. Working on the interview was a way of distracting himself. He had deliberately chosen the easiest question in order to take his mind off Charlotte. *And Josy.*

*What helped you cope?*

He didn't have to think about the answer. It consisted of one word: *alcohol.*

At first it was a sip or two, but the longer Josy was missing, the more it took to numb the pain. In the end he was drinking a full tumbler for every bad thought. Alcohol repressed the memories – and gave him some answers as well. More specifically, alcohol *was* the answer.

*Q: Would Josy be alive if I'd kept a closer eye on her?*

A: *Vodka.*

Q: *Why did I wait for half an hour in Dr Grohlke's clinic instead of sounding the alarm?*

A: *Absolut or Smirnoff. Doesn't matter so long as there's enough.*

Viktor leant back and stared at the ceiling. He was impatient to hear the end of Anna's story. There was still no news from Kai about the car crash, but he wasn't prepared to wait. He had to know what happened next. He needed more details, details that might reveal new connections, no matter how remote. And he needed a drink.

He chuckled again. It would be easy to convince himself that there were valid medical grounds for adding a dash of rum to his tea. Some varieties of alcohol were supposed to help against colds, but Viktor had left his trusted helpmates on the mainland and come to Parkum alone. Over the past few years most of his conversations had been conducted with Jim Beam and Jack Daniel's. In fact, he had come to depend on them so completely that his mind had been filled with a single obsessive thought: when could he call on them again?

Isabell had tried to intervene. She had talked to him, looked after him, commiserated with him, and pleaded with him.

When the angry phase was over, she did what anyone would advise an alcoholic's wife to do: she dropped him. Without so much as a goodbye, she upped and moved to a hotel. She didn't even call. He only noticed her absence when he ran out of supplies and felt too wretched to make the trip from the house, past the busy Wannsee lido, to the service station.

Then came the pain of sobriety – and with it, the memories.

Josy's first tooth.

Her birthdays.

Starting school.

Unwrapping a bike at Christmas.

Car journeys.

And Albert.

*Albert.*

Viktor gazed out of the window at the dark sea. He was so lost in thought that he didn't hear the light footsteps in the hall.

*Albert.*

If there was one reason why he had stopped drinking, it was him.

Back in the days when Viktor had a life and a job, he would leave the office at five o'clock and take the motor-way in the direction of Spanische Allee. Shortly after the Funkturm interchange he would pass the dilapidated grandstands that in times gone by had been packed with spectators enjoying an evening out at the Avus speedway, now converted into highway A115. As he drew level he would see an old man with an ancient ladies' bicycle standing by a gap in the fence. The old fellow waited in the same place almost every evening, gazing after the passing cars. It was the only section of motorway from Wedding to Potsdam that hadn't been blocked off by noise barriers and tall screens. And whenever Viktor hurtled past at a hundred kilometres per hour, he would find himself wondering why a person would be interested in watching the rear lights of car after car. Viktor never had time to look at him properly. He passed him on hundreds of occasions, but he was always driving too fast to make out the expression on his face. In spite of their almost daily encounters, he would never have recognized him on the street.

One evening, after a family outing to the Franco-German Volksfest in Reinickendorf, Josy noticed him too.

'What's he doing?' she asked, leaning round to watch through the rear window.

'He's confused,' was Isabell's phlegmatic response.

It didn't seem to satisfy Josy. 'I think he's called Albert,' she murmured softly, just loud enough for Viktor to hear.

'Why Albert?'

'Because he's lonely and old.'

'I see. And lonely old men are called Albert, are they?'

'Yes,' she said simply, and so it was settled. From then on, the old man was no longer a stranger and Viktor caught himself nodding at him as he drove home from work.

'Hello, Albert!'

Several years later, when he woke from an alcoholic stupor on the marble bathroom floor, it dawned on him that Albert was looking for something too. Whatever Albert had lost, he was obviously trying to find it in the stream of passing traffic. He and Albert were two of a kind. Viktor jumped into his Volvo and raced to the gap in the fence. Even from a distance he could tell that the old man wasn't there. He wasn't there the next day or the next day either. Albert was nowhere to be found.

Viktor knew exactly what he wanted to ask him. 'Excuse me, I was wondering what you were looking for. Have you lost someone too?'

But Albert steadfastly refused to show himself. He was gone.

*Like Josy.*

On the eighteenth day of driving to Albert's old haunt, Viktor gave up and drove home to start another bottle. Isabell was waiting at the door. She handed him a letter. It was from the editor of *Bunte*, requesting an interview.

'Dr Larenz?'

The voice scattered his thoughts. He stood up suddenly, ramming his right knee against the desk, then breathed in a mouthful of tea and spluttered frantically.

'Oh goodness,' said Anna who was standing right behind him. 'It's my fault, Doctor, I shouldn't have startled you again.' She stayed where she was, watching passively as he struggled for air. 'The door came open as soon as I knocked. I'm awfully sorry.'

Viktor knew full well that the door had been locked, but accepted her apology with a nod. He raised a hand to his head and realized that he was pouring with sweat.

'You look worse than yesterday, Doctor. I should probably go.'

He could feel her looking at him and he suddenly realized that he hadn't said a word.

'No, stay,' he said, his voice a little louder than intended.

Anna tilted her head to the side as if she hadn't fully understood.

'Stay,' he said again. 'I'll be fine. Take a seat. I'm glad you came. There's a couple of things I'd like to ask you.'

# 12

Anna took off her scarf and coat and made herself comfortable on the couch. Viktor returned to his usual position at the desk. He clicked his mouse and pretended to be scrolling through her case notes when really the information was saved in his head. It was just a ploy to buy himself time – he needed to steady his nerves if he was to quiz Anna about what she knew.

As he waited for his heart to slow to an acceptable rate, he realized it would take a supreme amount of concentration to focus on Anna's words. He was experiencing the kind of frazzled fatigue and achey lethargy that generally came from partying all night. Worse still, it felt as if the back of his skull was being squeezed in a vice. He clutched his head to stop the pounding and gazed at the sea.

The crashing waves were an inky blue, darkening by the minute as clouds accumulated overhead. Visibility was already restricted to two nautical miles and the horizon seemed to be creeping steadily closer to the shore.

Viktor studied Anna's reflection in the window. She poured herself a cup of tea and waited for him to begin.

He angled his chair towards her. 'I'd like to pick up where we left off, if I may.'

'Of course.'

Anna raised the delicate cup to her mouth and Viktor wondered whether her lipstick, a conservative shade of red, would leave a smudge on the Meissen china.

'You said that Charlotte left without telling her parents.'

'That's right.'

*My daughter wasn't a runaway*, thought Viktor. After pondering the matter all night, he had come to the conclusion that there had to be more to Josy's disappearance than a childish attempt to run away from home. *She simply wasn't the sort.*

'Charlotte set out on a quest to discover the cause of her illness,' said Anna. 'That's the gist of the story – or the opening twenty-three pages at least. A little girl falls ill, can't be cured, and runs away from home. That's as far as I got.'

'You said you weren't able to finish the story. Why do you think that was?'

'Just the usual, I'm afraid. I ran out of inspiration and abandoned the project. I saved the opening chapters in a folder on my computer and didn't give them another thought.'

'Until Charlotte showed up.'

'Exactly. Her appearance marked a turning point. I wasn't new to schizophrenia – I'd seen colours, heard voices, met characters from my stories, but Charlotte was different. This time the hallucination was incredibly real.'

*Because it wasn't a hallucination?*

Viktor raised his cup and wondered whether the bitter taste came from the tea or from the nasal spray that he was using to clear his catarrh. Even his taste buds had been affected by his cold.

'You said that Charlotte was nearly run over by a car.'

'Yes, that was the first time I saw her.'

'Where did you take her after that?'

'It was the other way round,' said Anna firmly. '*She* took me. I just followed.'

'How would you explain her motivation?'

'She wanted to know why her story only had two chapters. She said, "I want to be well again. What happens next?" She told me to finish the book.'

'In other words, you were instructed to keep writing by a character created by you?'

'Precisely. In any case, I was perfectly honest with her. I told her I didn't know how the story ended, so there was nothing I could do.'

'What did she say to that?'

'She took me by the hand and promised to show me where the story started. She said, "Maybe you'll think of an ending when you see where it all began."'

*Where what began?*

'Where did she take you?' he asked.

'I don't know the name of the place, but we drove for a while to get there. It was a bit of a blur.'

'Tell me in as much detail as you can.'

'We went back to my car and joined the motorway heading west. God knows which exit we took. The main thing I remember is that Charlotte was strapped in. Crazy, isn't it? My imaginary character was afraid of getting hurt. The absurdity of it struck me at the time.'

To Viktor, it made perfect sense. Josy had been taught by her mother to wear a seat belt at all times.

'How long did it take to get there?'

'Over an hour. We went through a little village. I remember seeing some old buildings – Russian architecture, I think.'

Viktor stiffened, waiting nervously for what he was about to hear. He was gripping his seat like a patient at the dentist's.

'There was a Russian Orthodox chapel on a hill in some woods. We crossed a bridge, continued for a couple of kilometres on the road, then turned on to a forest track.'

He listened incredulously. *No* ...

'We drove another kilometre and stopped in a narrow lane. I parked the car.'

*No, there's no way on earth that* ...

Viktor had to force himself not to leap out of his chair and shout at the top of his voice. He knew the place she was describing. He had driven there most weekends.

'Where did you go after that?'

'We walked down a path. We had to go in single file, but I could see she was taking me to a building. It was a little wooden house, like a cabin only nicer. It couldn't have been located in a more beautiful spot.'

*A log cabin in a clearing.* His thoughts were coming faster than Anna's words.

'It was the only house for miles. The forest went on forever; evergreens, beeches and birch. Some of the trees had shed their leaves, and there was a springy carpet of richly coloured autumn foliage on the ground. The weather was cold for November, but there was a cosiness to the place. At the time it seemed real, but everything was so luminously beautiful that I can't help wondering whether it was part of the delusion – like Charlotte.'

Viktor was wondering the same. It was hard to know which explanation would be preferable. Did he want Anna's hallucinations to be connected to his daughter's disappearance? Or was it better to think that the parallels were coincidental? He had to be careful about projecting his memories of Josy on to Anna's story. After all, the cabin she was describing wasn't necessarily his. There were scores of similar properties all over the Havelland.

He knew exactly how to find out.

'So you and Charlotte were standing outside the cabin. What could you hear?'

Anna looked at him doubtfully. 'Do you think it will help with my therapy?'

*No, but I need to know.*

'Yes,' he lied.

'Nothing. I couldn't hear a thing. I remember thinking how quiet it was. It was like being at the top of the tallest mountain with nothing for miles.'

Viktor acknowledged her answer with an earnest nod, barely controlling the urge to bang his head wildly like a heavy metal fan. It was exactly what he had expected her to say. He knew beyond a doubt where Charlotte had taken Anna. Sacrow Forest, midway between Spandau and Potsdam, was renowned for its tranquillity. The stillness was the first thing that city dwellers noticed about the place.

Anna seemed to guess his next question. 'I asked Charlotte where we were, but she obviously thought I should know. "Don't you recognize the house?" she said crossly. "We used to come here most weekends, especially in the summer. I had my last good day in this cabin – before it went wrong."'

'Before what went wrong?' probed Viktor.

'I assumed she was talking about her illness, but I didn't like to ask. The subject seemed to make her angry. "You're the novelist," she said irritably, pointing to the cabin. "Something happened in there, and it's your job to write it down!"'

'Did you?'

'I had to find out what had happened. Charlotte had made it clear that she intended to plague me until I finished the book, but I couldn't very well describe the cabin without going inside. I broke the glass in the back door and walked in.'

*Josy let her break into the cabin? Why didn't she use the spare key?*

'I thought I'd be able to find out what was making Charlotte ill.'

'And did you?'

'No. I didn't know what to look for. I was surprised by the size of the cabin. I was expecting to find three small rooms, but there was a spacious kitchen, two bathrooms, a lounge with a fireplace and a couple of bedrooms at least.'

*Three*, he corrected her silently.

'I went through all the cupboards and drawers – I looked everywhere, literally everywhere, including the toilet cistern. It didn't take long because the place was pretty bare. The furniture was expensive – but plain.'

*Isabell's choice: Philippe Starck and some quality Bauhaus.*

'Did Charlotte come with you?' asked Viktor.

'She refused to cross the threshold. Whatever had happened must have been really traumatic. I hunted about inside while she stood on the porch and shouted instructions.'

'Can you give me an example?'

'It was all a bit cryptic. She said things like, "Don't look for what you can see; search for what's missing!"'

'Did she explain what she meant?'

'No. I wanted to ask her, but there was no time for questions.'

'What happened?'

'I don't like to talk about it, Dr Larenz.'

'It's important to try.'

The hesitation in her eyes reminded Viktor of how she had clammed up completely the previous day.

'Can we talk about it tomorrow?' she said pleadingly. 'I want to go home.'

'That wouldn't be wise. It's better to get it over with.' He was shocked at himself for deceiving a patient. Anna had come to him for therapy, but this was an inquisition.

There was silence while Anna considered.

At first he was sure that she would stand up and leave, but then she placed her hands in her lap and sighed.

# 13

'I hadn't noticed the light was fading,' she continued, 'but suddenly I couldn't see a thing. It was probably only half past four – sundown was pretty early at that time of year. In any event, it was dark in the cabin, so I went back to the sitting room, borrowed a lighter from the mantelpiece and used the radiance from the small flame to light my way down the hall. At the far end was a door I hadn't noticed before. It looked like a broom cupboard or something.'

*Josy's room.*

'I wanted to take a closer look, but then I heard voices.'

'What sort of voices?'

'Actually, it was a single voice, a man's voice. He wasn't talking; he was crying. It sounded as if he was whimpering to himself. The noise was coming from the room at the end of the hall.'

'How could you tell?'

'The whimpering got louder as I approached.'

'Weren't you frightened?'

'I managed to stay calm for a bit, but then Charlotte started screaming.'

'Why?' asked Viktor hoarsely. He could feel the rawness in his throat when he talked.

'She wanted me to leave. She was yelling at the top of her voice, "He's coming! He's coming!"'

'Who did she mean?'

'I don't know. In the same moment that Charlotte started shouting, the whimpering stopped. I was right outside the door and the handle was moving. I felt a draught and the lighter went out. Then a terrifying thought occurred to me.'

'What?'

'The danger that Charlotte was warning me about had been there all along.'

The telephone rang. Viktor, who was itching to ask the next question, hurried to the kitchen to take the call. The touch-tone phone had been installed at Isabell's insistence. She refused to stay in a house without a modern phone.

'Hi. I'm not sure whether this is good news or bad,' said Kai without preamble.

'Just be quick,' whispered Viktor, not wanting Anna to overhear.

'OK, the traffic accident: I put one of my best fellows on it, and I made a few enquiries myself. We know two things for certain. First, a couple of cars rear-ended on Uhlandstrasse on the afternoon of November 26.'

Viktor's heart missed a beat, only to speed up alarmingly.

'Second, it had nothing to do with your daughter's abduction.'

'What makes you so sure?'

'A guy stumbled into the road and nearly got run over. According to the witnesses, he was drunk. There was no sign of any kid.'

'You're saying that . . .'

'I'm saying that schizophrenic or not, your patient had nothing to do with our problem.'

'Josy isn't a problem.'

'No, of course not. I'm sorry, Viktor. I didn't mean it that way.'

'It's all right, Kai, I shouldn't have taken offence. I just thought we were finally getting somewhere.'

'I know how distressing this is for you.'

*No you don't*, thought Viktor. He wouldn't wish that fate on anyone. Kai had no idea what it was like to lose everything, to feel so wretched that every glimmer of hope seemed dazzlingly bright.

'Did they find the guy?'

'Which guy?'

'The drunk guy. Did they question him?'

'No, but that doesn't change the fact that no one saw a woman or a kid. The same facts came up in all the witness statements: a drunk man staggered across the road and disappeared into the car park at the Kudamm-Karree mall. He was gone before anyone asked for his details. You know how crowded it gets in those superstores. Who's to say that he wasn't buying himself a—'

'It's all right, Kai, I understand. I appreciate your help, but I should probably go now.'

'Is your mental patient there?'

'Yes. She's in the other room.'

'You've been cross-examining her again, haven't you?'

'Yes.'

'I might have guessed. Well you can leave me out of it. Next you'll be telling me that you've found a new lead. I suppose you've found some more parallels?'

'Maybe.'

'OK, Doc, here's what happens next. You throw her out. Whoever she is, she's not doing you any good. You said you were going to Parkum to get some peace. You should be looking after yourself, not her. There are plenty of other shrinks who could help her.'

'I can't send her back to the mainland until the weather clears up. And I can't just throw her out!'

'Then tell her not to bother you any more.'

Viktor knew that Kai was right. He had left Berlin in the hope of getting closure, but Josy was still at the forefront of his mind. And there were parts of Anna's story that didn't make sense. He had heard what he wanted to hear and forgotten about the rest. Josy was twelve, not nine. She wasn't the type to run away from home, and she knew where to find the key to the cabin. She wouldn't let a stranger vandalize their door.

'Well?'

Viktor was brought back to reality by the sound of Kai's voice. 'Well what?'

'Remember what you promised? *I* check out the car accident, and *you* call off the hunt. You need to stop looking for her, Viktor. You're only opening old wounds.'

'Sure, but—'

'We had a deal.'

'Just hear me out,' said Viktor coldly.

'What?'

'There aren't any old wounds; only fresh ones. They haven't healed.'

# 14

Viktor replaced the receiver quietly and made his way unsteadily to the sitting room, swaying slightly as if he were on a boat.

'Bad news?'

Anna had got to her feet and was preparing to leave.

'I'm not sure,' he said truthfully. 'Are you off?'

'Yes, I need to lie down for an hour or so. I think I underestimated how draining these sessions would be. Can I come back tomorrow?'

'Yes. I mean, *maybe*.'

Viktor was still figuring out how to respond to Kai's advice.

'I might be busy tomorrow. Why don't you give me a call? Technically, I'm not supposed to be seeing patients, and I'm behind with my other work.'

'Of course.'

Viktor felt sure that Anna was studying his expression and wondering what had prompted his reversal of mood. But she was too polite, or too canny, to let it show.

As soon as she was out of the house, he picked up his palmtop to find the number of the hotel where his wife was staying in New York. He was still scrolling through his contact list when the telephone rang for the second time that day.

'One more thing, Viktor.'

*Kai.*

'This isn't about the other business.' He stopped and corrected himself. 'I mean, it's got nothing to do with Josy. I just thought you'd want to fix it before the weather makes things worse.'

'Fix what?'

'I had a call from the alarm company. They couldn't get hold of anyone in Schwanenwerder so they tried me instead.'

'Oh God, we've been burgled.'

'Not exactly. As far as we know, nothing was taken. And your villa is just as you left it, don't worry.'

'Then what's the problem?'

'Someone broke into your cabin in Sacrow. The glass was smashed at the back.'

# 15

Viktor was watching him. As the crow flies, there were four hundred and sixty-two kilometres between them, including a stretch of water measuring fifty nautical miles, but Viktor was following his every move. He tracked Kai Strathmann's progress through the cabin. The background noise on his phone was all he needed to pinpoint his exact location. The PI had driven to Sacrow with orders to inspect the damage to the cabin – and check out Anna's story.

'OK, I'm in the kitchen.'

The sound of Kai's squeaking trainers carried all the way from Sacrow to Parkum as a series of electrical pulses.

'Well?' said Viktor impatiently. 'Has anything been touched?' He jammed the receiver between his shoulder and chin, picked up the ancient dial phone and took a couple of steps away from the desk. The cord ran out before he reached the couch, so he hovered in the middle of the room.

'If you ask me, no one's been here for ages. I'd give those surfaces a wipe before you invite any guests.'

'We haven't been to the cabin in four years,' said

Viktor pointedly. He knew that Kai would be regretting his witticisms.

'That's understandable, Doc.'

The short walk through the woods had taken its toll on the 120-kilo PI. He was careful to hold his mobile away from his mouth, but Viktor could hear him wheezing all the same.

'Nothing to report except the broken window. Judging by the evidence, it had nothing to do with Josy, whatever your mental patient tells you.'

'What makes you say that?'

'The damage is too recent. We're talking days, not months – and definitely not years.'

'How do you know? Can you tell from the shards?' Viktor raised his voice to cover the sound of banging doors. Kai was going through the cupboards and the fridge.

'Viktor, there's a bloody great hole in the door. I'd expect to see damage to the floorboards – snow, rain, leaves, not to mention hordes of insects. There isn't a mark or stain in sight. Just a thick layer of dust, same as everywh—'

'Thank you, Kai, I get the picture.'

Viktor, whose arms were beginning to ache, walked the telephone back to the coffee table.

'Charlotte apparently asked my patient to "search for what's missing". I'd like you to check if anything's been stolen.'

'Anything in particular? A Picasso? A kitchen whisk?

How am I supposed to know what's missing? I'd need a whole bloody inventory. By the way, there aren't any beers in the fridge, if that's what you mean.'

'We'll start with Josy's room,' said Viktor, ignoring Kai's banter. 'It's at the end of the hall by the bathroom.'

'I'm on my way.'

Kai's trainers had stopped squeaking now that he was out of the kitchen and walking down the tiled hall. Viktor closed his eyes and counted the fifteen paces that the PI would take to reach Josy's door.

'Come in!' said the sign that Kai would see when he looked for the handle. In a moment he would be shining his torch around the room. A creaking of hinges confirmed that he was there.

'OK, I'm in.'

'Well?'

'I've got my back to the hall and I'm looking into the room. Everything looks normal.'

'Tell me what you can see.'

'Just the usual. Canopy bed – the curtains could definitely do with a wash. Fluffy rug on the floor, now home to a colony of mites. They're probably to blame for the smell.'

'Anything else?'

'A big framed poster of Ernie and Bert. It's on the opposite wall to the bed.'

'Ernie and Bert. They were . . .'

Viktor wiped the tears from his right eye and fell silent. He didn't want Kai to hear the quiver in his voice.

*They were a present from me.*

'*Sesame Street*, I know. Looking left, there's a shelf – Ikea, if I'm not mistaken. Do you want me to list the toys? A Steiff elephant, a couple of Disney characters—'

'Wait! Back up a bit,' said Viktor.

'What?'

'I've just remembered something. Can you lie on the bed?'

'If it makes you happy – yes.'

Three footsteps, some rustling and a cough. Kai's voice came through the phone.

'I hope it stands the strain. The mattress is protesting already.'

'Pay attention, Kai. I'd like you to tell me what you see.'

'OK, to my left I've got a window. I'm assuming the forest is out there somewhere but it's time you cleaned the glass. And like I said, the poster is staring right at me.'

'Is that all?'

'Well, from this angle, the shelf is on the right and—'

'No,' Viktor stopped him. 'Is there anything else *in front* of you?'

'Nope. And if you don't mind...' The phone line crackled, swallowing the next few words. 'I ... bloody bed, OK?'

'OK.'

'Listen, Viktor, I've had enough of this lark. Why don't you tell me what you're looking for?'

'Give me a moment.'

Viktor closed his eyes and focused on the cabin. A moment later he was walking through the forest to the door. He walked up the steps, took off his shoes and put them in the hand-carved Indian cabinet in the hall. He glanced into the parlour where Isabell was lying on the white Rolf Benz sofa beside the fireplace, reading the latest issue of *Gala* magazine. He breathed in the aroma of burning pine and enjoyed the sensation of being in a house whose warmth was derived from the contentment of its occupants. Music was coming from the rear of the house. Taking off his coat, he went to find Josy. The music got louder as he approached. He pushed down the handle, opened the door, and was blinded by the sunlight streaming through the window. Then he saw her. She was sitting at her kid-sized dressing table, trying out some orange nail polish belonging to one of her friends. She hadn't heard him come in because of the music. It was coming from the television, which was tuned to . . .

'I thought you were going to tell me what to look for,' said Kai, cutting through his thoughts. Viktor opened his eyes.

*MTV.*

'A television.'

'A television?'

'Yes, a Sony.'

'No, no sign of a telly.'

'And a dressing table with a round mirror.'

'Ditto – unless it's in another room.'

'That's it then.'

'A dressing table and a telly? I'm sorry, Viktor, but it doesn't sound like your average burglary.'

'Because it wasn't,' retorted Viktor, more certain than ever that Anna and Josy were linked. *Don't ask me how, but I'm going to find out.*

'Either way, you've been burgled. Don't you think we should call the police?'

'No, not yet. If you've finished in Josy's room, I'd like you to check the rest of the house.'

'I guess so . . .' There was a rustling noise at the end of the phone, and Viktor deduced that Kai was scratching his head, probably towards the back where he still had a respectable amount of hair.

'What?'

'It probably sounds stupid, but . . .'

'I'm listening, Kai.'

'All right, if you want to know what I think, the room is missing more than the odd piece of furniture.'

'I beg your pardon?'

The PI cleared his throat nervously. 'Josy was twelve, right?'

'What's that got to do with anything?'

'The atmosphere isn't right. I've been in this game for long enough to trust my instincts. And my instincts are telling me that this isn't a twelve-year-old's room.'

'Can you be more specific?'

'I don't have kids myself, but a niece of mine, Laura, is about to turn thirteen. The sign on her door doesn't say "Come in!" Quite the opposite in fact. Last time I went round there, she banned us all from her room.'

'Josy was a good kid. She wasn't rebellious.'

'I'm not talking about being rebellious; I'm talking about a normal teenage room. Boy band posters on the walls, signed tickets from pop concerts stuck to the mirror, postcards from the boys at school ... Do you see what I'm getting at?'

*Something's missing.*

'Quite honestly, no.'

'What I'm saying is that no self-respecting adolescent would want to live in a room like this. Where are the copies of *Bravo* magazine? I mean, honestly, Viktor, whoever heard of a twelve-year-old watching *Sesame Street*? My niece is into Eminem, not Ernie and Bert!'

'Who's Eminem?'

'Precisely my point. He's a rapper. I'll tell you about his lyrics another time.'

'I still don't see your point.'

'You asked if anything was missing, and I'm telling you, *yes*. I'd expect to see a locked box of love letters. I'd expect to see a candle in a wine bottle with wax dripping down the side. And you're absolutely right: I'd expect to see a dressing table.'

'But a moment ago you said everything looked normal.'

'Sure, if we're talking about an eight-year-old's room. Josy was twelve.'

'We only came here at weekends, remember. Most of her belongings were in Berlin.'

'You're the one who asked,' said Kai with a sigh. 'I was only giving you my opinion.'

Viktor heard him close the bedroom door. With that, his vision of the cabin in Sacrow disappeared. It was as if the projector had burnt out halfway through the film.

'Where are you going?'

'Sorry, Doc, I've got to pee. I'll call you back.'

Before Viktor could protest, the audio connection was lost as well. Kai had rung off.

Rooted to the spot, Viktor waited by the telephone and struggled to make sense of it all.

He went back over the facts. Someone had broken into the cabin within the last few days. And Josy was too old for her room.

He couldn't ponder the matter any further because he had to answer the phone. He hadn't expected Kai to call back so soon.

'Viktor?'

Judging by the background noise, the PI had left the cabin and was standing in the woods.

'Hang on, you can't leave yet! We haven't been through the other rooms. I wanted to ask you to—'

'Viktor!' The detective sounded agitated. There was an unmistakable note of panic in his voice.

'What's wrong?' asked Viktor, alarmed.

'I'm calling the police.'

'Why? What's happened?'

*Josy.*

'I've found evidence in the bathroom. Someone was here this afternoon.'

'For Christ's sake, Kai, what kind of evidence?'

'Blood on the tiles, in the basin, in the loo.' He took a deep breath.

'Viktor, the whole place is covered in blood.'

# 16

## *Room 1245, Berlin-Wedding Psychosomatic Clinic*

Dr Roth's bleep went off just as Viktor paused for the first time in his hour-long account.

'Remember where you're up to, Doctor,' said the psychiatrist, unlocking the heavy door. He disappeared into the corridor to use the telephone on the ward.

*As if I could forget*, thought Viktor. *God knows I've tried to get rid of the memories.* Forgetting was what he aspired to; it would be a release.

Two minutes later, Dr Roth was back by his bedside. He sat down on an uncomfortable folding contraption made of white plastic. It was the first time such a chair, a common enough sight in the other wards, had been positioned by this particular bed. The patients assigned to room 1245 rarely received visitors of any kind.

'Good news and bad news,' reported the psychiatrist.

'I'll have the bad news first.'

'Professor Malzius wants to know where I am. He's getting impatient.'

'And the good news?'

'You have visitors coming – but they won't be here until six.'

Viktor merely nodded. He had a fair idea as to who the visitors would be, and Roth's expression seemed to confirm his hunch.

'That gives us forty minutes.'

'Forty minutes for you to tell me exactly what happened.'

Larenz stretched his limbs as far as the restraints allowed.

'Bed-bound at the age of forty-seven,' he said smilingly, jangling the straps around his wrists and ankles. Dr Roth pretended not to hear. He knew what Viktor was hinting at, but he couldn't oblige.

'So your cabin had been broken into. Why didn't you call the police?' he asked, picking up where they had left off.

'The police had been working on the case for four years and found nothing. I knew I was getting somewhere and I didn't want them to mess things up.'

Dr Roth nodded sympathetically. 'Meanwhile, you were stuck on Parkum and Kai was your only point of contact with the outside world.'

'Yes.'

'How long did the situation continue like that? When did you realize who Anna was and what had happened to Josy?'

'Two days. I should have realized sooner. The trouble was, to see the truth I needed to press rewind – to play

102

back the tape and go over what had happened – but I was too busy looking ahead. If I'd stopped for a moment, I would have noticed that the solution to the puzzle was obvious.'

'And Kai had just told you that your bathroom was covered in blood.'

'Yes.'

'What happened after that?'

'It was dark by then, so I couldn't do much except pack. I was planning to leave the island on the next available ferry. I wanted to meet up with Kai and get a handle on the situation. As it turned out, I was forced to stay. The winds had picked up overnight and my cold had taken control over my body. Can you imagine what it feels like to be sunburned all over?'

Dr Roth nodded.

'That's how it was. On commercials, it's described as "muscle pain and general discomfort", but there's always one part of the body that soldiers on.'

'The mind, I suppose.'

'Right. I needed to get some rest, so I took a couple of Valium and prayed for the weather to improve.'

'But the ferry couldn't sail?'

'No, I was trapped by Hurricane Anton. The coastguard issued a special warning to the residents of Parkum, advising us to stay inside except in an emergency. But in my case, the emergency was already underway.'

'Another problem?'

'A disappearance – and in my own house, as well.'

'Who was it this time?'

Viktor lifted his head a little and frowned. 'Before we go any further, I'd like to propose a deal. I'll tell you the rest of the story on one condition.'

'What?'

'You give me my freedom.'

Dr Roth smiled a tight-lipped smile and blew air through his nose. They had discussed the matter already. 'You know I can't do that – not after your confession. Not only would I lose my job and my licence, I could be sent to prison as well.'

'I know, you made yourself clear the first time. I'll just have to take the risk.'

'What risk?'

'I'm going to tell you the story, the whole story, and when I'm finished, you can decide what to do.'

'Dr Larenz, surely you realize that it's out of my hands. I'm here to listen to you, to talk to you, but I'm not in a position to help – regardless of how often you ask.'

'Very well. As I said, I'm willing to take that risk. Listen to the rest of the story and maybe you'll change your mind.'

'I wouldn't bet on it.'

Viktor wanted to raise his hands soothingly, but he was tied to the bed. 'We'll see.'

He closed his eyes and Dr Roth leant back in his chair to listen to the next chapter in the story – the next chapter in Viktor's tragedy.

# 17

**Two days before the truth, Parkum**

The effect of the tablets had worn off and Viktor was yanked from his dreamless sleep. He wanted to linger in the pain-free vacuum that the Valium had created for him, but the drug had loosened its numbing hold on his consciousness and dark thoughts permeated his brain.

*Anna.*

*Charlotte.*

*Josy.*

*The blood on the bathroom floor ...*

Viktor sat up slowly and nearly flopped back against the pillows. The sudden heaviness of his body reminded him of a diving trip in the Bahamas years earlier with Isabell. They had both been wearing buoyancy compensators, and he hadn't noticed the weight of the equipment until it came to climbing back into the boat and he suddenly seemed to weigh a thousand tons. He was experiencing a similar drag on his body now, but this time the Valium, or maybe his influenza, was to blame.

*A fine mess you're in,* he thought, summoning the strength to stumble out of bed. *Now you don't know whether you're in this state because of the pills or because you're really ill.*

He felt shivery in his sweat-drenched pyjamas, so he took a silk dressing gown from a hook on the door and pulled it over his shoulders. Then he set off shakily in the direction of the bathroom, which – mercifully for him – was only a few metres away. He didn't have to tackle the stairs – at least, not yet.

He was shocked to see his own reflection. Now he knew for certain that he was ill. Glazed, lifeless eyes, tired features, pale, greyish skin, and beads of sweat on his forehead. But that was only part of the problem.

*I can sense something's wrong.*

He stared at his reflection and tried to lock gazes with himself. It didn't work. The more he focused on the mirror, the blearier his reflection became.

'Bloody pills,' he mumbled, reaching into the cubicle to turn on the shower. He shunted the lever to the left and pulled it up, leaving the water to run. As usual, the ancient generator took ages to heat the water, but at least he didn't have to listen to Isabell complaining about the waste.

Viktor leant over the marble basin and peered at the mirror again. He felt a numbing tiredness come over him. The drumming of the water in the shower seemed to reinforce the gloominess of his thoughts.

*I can sense something's wrong, but what? It's all so …*
*hazy.*

He dragged himself away from his reflection, hung a towel on the shower door, and stepped into the steamy glass cabinet. The sharp aroma of Acqua di Parma cleared his nostrils and gave him a boost. He finished his shower feeling considerably improved. The warm jet of water had blasted away the outer layer of pain and washed it down the plughole. If only it were able to take away his thoughts.

*I know something's wrong, something's different.* He couldn't work it out.

Viktor rummaged through the closet and pulled out a pair of old Levi's and a blue roll-neck top. He knew Anna would probably pay him a visit; in fact, he wanted her to come so he could hear the next instalment of Charlotte's story, or maybe even the end. But it was too much effort to dress for the occasion. She would have to put up with him in his casual clothes – not that she was likely to care.

Viktor negotiated the stairs, gripping the wooden banister just in case. He went into the kitchen, filled the electric kettle, fetched a teabag from the cupboard and chose a big-bellied mug from the row of wooden hooks between the sink and the oven. He sat with his back to the rain-streaked window, ignoring the dark clouds gathering ominously over Parkum, and tried to focus on his breakfast. But his thoughts refused to submit to the morning routine.

*Something's missing. What is it?*

He stood up to fetch the milk and caught a glimpse of his reflection in the glass-ceramic stove top. He looked even blearier, so bleary that his face seemed distorted. And then he realized what was wrong.

*Gone!*

His eyes moved down the stove and swept the individually laid marble tiles.

He was seized by the same awful feeling, the feeling of apprehension that had taken hold of him yesterday while he was guiding Kai through the cabin in Sacrow.

He dropped his cup and ran into the hall. Tearing open the door to the sitting room, he stormed towards his desk.

A stack of files, the printout of the email from *Bunte*, the open laptop. Everything was there.

*No, something was missing.*

Viktor closed his eyes, hoping that everything would be back to normal when he opened them again. But he hadn't been mistaken. Nothing had changed when he next surveyed the room.

He bent down and peered beneath the desk. *Nothing*.

Sindbad was gone.

He ran back to the kitchen and scanned the room.

*Nothing*.

There was no sign of Sindbad. His feeding bowl was missing, as were the tins of dog food, his water bowl and the blanket beneath the desk. It was almost as if the retriever had never entered the house. But Viktor was too frantic to notice.

# 18

He stood on the beach, rain streaming down his face, and tried to marshal his thoughts. Strangely enough, he wasn't completely distraught. Sad, yes, but not beside himself with grief. Since losing Josy, he had lived in fear of a catastrophe such as this. First his daughter, then his dog. Both had vanished without trace.

The double blow was precisely why he had never advised a grieving patient to think about getting a pet. All too often, heartbroken husbands and wives would try to replace their loved ones with a dog, only for the precious animal to be run over by a car.

*Missing or dead.*

Sindbad was nowhere to be seen. Viktor marvelled again at his composure. So far, he hadn't suffered a nervous breakdown, run screaming through the village, or knocked on all the neighbours' doors. He had simply left a message on Halberstaedt's answerphone and hurried outside to look for Sindbad on the beach. Now, two hundred and fifty metres or so from the cottage, he was poking about in the driftwood. There was no sign of the golden retriever's tracks; perhaps there never had been.

'Sindbad!'

He was wasting his breath. For one thing, the dog couldn't hear him; and for another, he certainly wouldn't obey. Sindbad took fright so easily that innocent noises, such as unexpected splutters from the hearth, were almost the death of him. Firecrackers were a thousand times worse: Isabell had to mix tranquillizers into Sindbad's food on New Year's Eve. And Sindbad had once run all the way from Grunewald to Schwanenwerder after hearing a single gunshot in the woods. Viktor and Isabell had bellowed and whistled to no avail.

The roar of the waves was enough to frighten a braver dog than Sindbad, and Viktor wondered how he had summoned the courage to leave the house. It didn't make sense, especially since the doors had been locked.

Viktor had checked the whole cottage, scouring the rooms from basement to attic. Nothing. The generator shed was padlocked on the outside, but he had searched it all the same. He was aware that retrievers weren't capable of picking locks, but then where else could Sindbad be? *He must be somewhere on the island.* Unless . . .

Viktor spun round and scanned the length of the coast. He felt a brief wave of elation as he detected a slight movement on the landward side of the beach. Something was approaching and it was big enough to be a dog. But his hopes were dashed a moment later. The creature was too dark to be a golden retriever. And it was a person, not a dog. A woman in a dark coat.

Anna.

'It's good to see you getting some fresh air,' she called

from a distance of ten or so metres. The wind tore holes in her speech, casting some of the syllables out to sea. It was hard to hear what she was saying. 'Not many people would venture out in weather like this.'

'I'd be inside if I had the choice,' he shouted, suddenly aware of the inflammation in his throat. Sindbad's disappearance had made him forget about his ailments.

'Why? Is something wrong?' She stopped a few paces away from him, and Viktor was astonished to see that her patent shoes were impeccably clean. He wondered how she had managed to negotiate the track from the village without muddying her feet.

'I'm looking for my dog.'

'Your dog?' said Anna, anchoring her headscarf with her right hand. 'I didn't know you had one.'

'You must have seen him – a great big golden retriever. He was lying under the desk.'

Anna shook her head. 'No, I can't say I noticed a dog.'

Her strange denial hit Viktor with greater force than the hurricane. There was a ringing noise in his right ear, and the emptiness inside him gave way to paralysing fear.

He remembered Halberstaedt's warning. *There's something funny about that woman.*

Raindrops were catching in his eyebrows and splashing into his eyes. Anna's face became a blur. Snatches of their first conversation surfaced in his memory.

*I battered him to a pulp. He didn't even look like a dog when I was finished.*

Viktor was too busy worrying about Anna's lies and violent hallucinations to listen to what she was saying. He suddenly realized that her lips were moving. 'Did you say something, Ms Glass?'

'We should probably go inside,' she repeated more loudly, nodding towards the house. 'I'm sure your dog won't stay out in this weather.' She reached for his hand.

Viktor stepped back a little too hastily and nodded. 'You're probably right.'

He led the way slowly towards the house.

*How could anyone fail to notice a big dog like Sindbad?* He wondered why Anna would lie to him. *What if she had something to do with Sindbad's disappearance as well as Josy's?*

Had Viktor been less preoccupied with his own thoughts, he might have remembered the first piece of advice given to him by his mentor and friend Professor van Druisen: 'Always focus on the patient. Listen carefully to what he or she has to say, and keep an open mind.'

Instead of that, Viktor was wearing himself out in a futile attempt to repress the clues that were surfacing from his unconscious. The truth was already visible. It lay before him, helpless and desperate like a drowning man in a frozen lake. But Viktor Larenz refused to punch through the thin layer of ice.

He still wasn't ready.

# 19

'We ran.'

The conversation had taken a while to get going. Viktor, incapable of thinking about anything but Sindbad, had zoned out during the first few minutes, and when he finally started listening, he was relieved to discover that she hadn't said anything new. Anna was still recapping the story: she and Charlotte had driven to a forest, and Charlotte had waited while Anna broke into a cabin and heard a man crying in one of the rooms.

'What were you running from?' asked Viktor eventually.

'I didn't stop to think. I just sensed that whatever had been hiding in the cabin was coming after us. I grabbed Charlotte's hand and we ran through the snow to the car. Neither of us dared to look back. We were frightened of what was behind us, and the path was quite slippery so we had to watch our step.'

'Who was in the cabin? Who was following you?'

'I can't say for sure. My first priority was to get Charlotte into the car, lock the doors and head back to Berlin. As soon as we were on the road, I tried to get some answers, but Charlotte was talking in riddles.'

'Can you remember what she said?'

'Things like: "I'm not here to give you answers. I'll show you the clues, but I can't explain their meaning. You're the one who's writing this story, not me."'

Viktor was forced to concede that Anna's story was becoming increasingly fanciful, which wasn't entirely surprising in view of her mental health. He only hoped that her imaginings bore some relation, no matter how tenuous, to the truth. At the same time he couldn't help but realize that his attitude towards her delusions was slightly pathological. He decided not to care.

'Where was she taking you?'

'To see the next clue. She said, "You've seen where everything started. It's time I showed you something else."'

'The first clue was the cabin in the forest?'

'Yes.'

'So what happened next?'

'Charlotte said something really strange, something I'll never forget.' Anna pressed her lips together and spoke in the whispered voice of a young girl. '"I want to show you where the illness lives."'

'Where it *lives*?'

'That's what she said.'

Viktor shivered. He hadn't warmed up since coming in from the beach, and Anna's unnaturally childish voice seemed to lower his temperature by a couple of degrees.

'Where did you go?' he persisted. 'Did you find the illness?'

'We drove back to Berlin via the Glienicke Bridge

with Charlotte giving me directions. I can't remember the rest of the route. For one thing, I'm not familiar with that part of the city – and besides, I couldn't concentrate because Charlotte had taken a turn for the worse.'

Viktor felt a lurching sensation in his stomach. 'What was the matter with her?'

'It started with a nosebleed. We were near the lido on Lake Wannsee at the time. I parked outside a beer garden and Charlotte lay down in the back. The nosebleed stopped, but a moment later . . .'

*She started shaking.*

'. . . she started shaking all over. She was shivering so violently that I wanted to rush her to hospital.' She gave a forced laugh. 'But then I remembered she didn't exist. A visit to the doctor's was hardly going to help.'

'So you did nothing?'

'To be honest, I thought it was best. It seemed foolish to pander to my hallucinations, but Charlotte kept getting worse. She was shivering all over and begging me to take her to the pharmacy.'

*She needed penicillin.*

'She wanted antibiotics, but I knew it was hopeless: we needed a prescription. I tried to explain that to Charlotte, but the tantrums started. I couldn't calm her down.'

'Did she shout at you?'

'She was shouting, crying and screaming at the top of her lungs. It was dreadful to listen to her hoarse little voice.'

'What kind of things was she saying?'

SEBASTIAN FITZEK

'She blamed me for creating her. I remember her yelling, "You gave me this illness; you need to make me well!" I knew I was hallucinating and she didn't exist, but it was no good – I couldn't ignore her. In the end, I drove to the pharmacy, bought some paracetamol for her headache and charmed the guy behind the counter into dispensing the penicillin. He handed me the tablets and told me to come back with the prescription as soon as I could. If I'm honest with myself, I was doing it for my own good and not to help Charlotte: I knew I wouldn't get rid of my hallucinations unless I did what she said.'

'Did it work?'

'Things improved for me, but not for Charlotte.'

Viktor nodded and waited for her to explain.

'Charlotte took two tablets, but I don't think they helped. If anything, she got worse, not better. She looked pale and listless, but at least she stopped screaming. I guess I was still in shock, though, because I can't remember how we got to the villa by the lake.'

'But you remember the villa?'

'It was stunning, simply stunning. I've never seen such a beautiful house in Berlin. It didn't seem to belong in the city – it was more like a country estate. The grounds must have covered a few thousand square metres at least, and the lawn sloped down to the water's edge. There was a private beach and a jetty, and the house itself was huge. As far as I could tell, the architecture was neoclassical with a few extravagant flourishes – oriels, turrets and the like. No wonder Charlotte called it a "palace".'

*Schwanenwerder.*

Once again Anna's description was uncannily accurate. Viktor had heard enough to know that she was definitely involved.

'The house and the gardens were impressive enough, but I hadn't reckoned with the commotion outside. The whole place was swarming with people and cars. We had to get out and walk a couple of hundred metres over a little bridge because the road was chock-a-block with vans.'

'Vans?'

'Right. They were parked bumper-to-bumper. Everyone seemed to be heading . . .'

*. . . towards my house . . .*

'. . . in the same direction as us. The road was really narrow and we had to push our way through. A big crowd had gathered on the pavement at the end of the drive. No one noticed our arrival. In fact, they were all too busy staring at the house. Some were using binoculars, others had telephoto lenses. Barely a second went by without a mobile phone or a camera flash going off. A couple of men had climbed a tree to get a better view, but they couldn't compete with the helicopter circling overhead.'

Viktor knew the exact location of the house. What was more, he could practically pinpoint the date of their visit. In the days following Josy's disappearance, the media had laid siege to his villa in Schwanenwerder, placing an intolerable strain on Isabell and himself.

'Suddenly a cry went up from the crowd. The front door opened and someone stepped outside.'

'Who?'

'I couldn't tell. We were standing at the top of the drive, seven or eight hundred metres from the house. I tried asking Charlotte who lived there, but she avoided the question. "It's my house," she told me. "I grew up here." Then I asked why she had brought me there, and she said, "Don't you get it? I live in this place – and the illness lives here too."'

'The illness?'

'That's what she said. From what I could gather, something in the house was making her ill. That's why she left home – firstly, to establish the cause of her illness, and secondly, to break free.'

*So Josy's illness was caused by something in Schwanenwerder.*

'I was still deciding what to make of it all when she tugged on my sleeve and begged me to go. I ignored her at first because I wanted to get a proper look at the person on the drive. I still didn't know if it was a man or a woman, but whoever it was looked vaguely familiar and I wanted to stay. But then Charlotte said something that changed my mind.'

'Well?'

'She said: "We need to go. Remember the thing in the cabin? It followed us – and it's here."'

# 20

'May I use your bathroom?'

Anna had clearly decided to take a break from her story. She stood up briskly.

He nodded. 'Of course.' Not for the first time it struck him that Anna was unusually well spoken. It was almost as if she were compensating for the awfulness of her narrative by carefully enunciating each word.

He wanted to rise to his feet, but a dead weight was pushing on his shoulders, keeping him down.

'The bathroom is—'

'Upstairs and second on the left – I know.'

He gaped at her in disbelief, but she was already in the doorway and didn't turn round.

*She knew where the bathroom was? How?*

His plan of sitting and waiting was abandoned. Summoning his strength, he hauled himself upright, walked to the door, and stopped. A pool of water had formed on the floor where Anna's cashmere coat, dripping wet from her walk in the rain, was draped over a chair by the couch. He picked it up to move it to the hall and was surprised by its weight. The waterlogged cashmere couldn't account for the heaviness. He checked the silk lining: *bone dry*. There had to be another explanation.

Viktor heard a door close upstairs and a bolt shoot home. Anna was safely in the bathroom.

He gave the coat a little shake and traced the clunking noise to the right-hand pocket. Without really thinking, he thrust his hand inside. The pocket seemed virtually bottomless and Viktor was on the point of giving up when his fingers met with a handkerchief and, a few centimetres later, a large wallet. He whipped it out and weighed it in his hand: an *Aigner* wallet from the men's collection. He thought of Anna and her beautifully coordinated, ladylike style. What would she want with a man's wallet?

*Who is this woman?*

Upstairs, the toilet flushed. Since the bathroom was almost directly above the sitting room, Viktor could hear the clacking of high-heeled shoes on the marble floor, from which he deduced that Anna was standing at the basin. As if on cue, he heard a squeaking of taps and a tumbling of water through the ancient copper pipes.

Time was running out. He flipped open the wallet and checked the plastic pocket at the front. No ID; no driving licence. His heart slowed to a crawl as he realized that his discovery, far from solving the enigma of Anna's identity, only added to the mystery. She wasn't carrying a single bank card or even any cash – at least not in notes.

Viktor suddenly lost his nerve and his hands began to shake. The tremor was only slight, but he couldn't control it. In the past, it had always been a physiological response to a dip in blood alcohol, but this time it wasn't the drink that was making him jittery. The silence was to blame. Anna had turned off the taps.

He closed the wallet quickly and picked up Anna's coat. Just then the telephone rang, and he stumbled back guiltily, dropping the wallet that he should never have touched. It hit the floor with a thud, landing in the expectant pause between two rings. And Viktor, watching in frozen horror, learned the secret of its heaviness: coins were spilling in all directions, rolling across the parquet floor as if propelled by an invisible hand.

*Damn.*

Upstairs, the bathroom door opened. Viktor knew it was only a matter of seconds before Anna got back to the sitting room and found the contents of her wallet on the floor.

Dropping to his knees, he scrabbled after the spinning coins, snatching at them with trembling hands. Meanwhile, the phone was ringing in the background, and his fingernails were too short, his hands too unsteady and the floor too slippery to get any leverage on the coins.

And so he knelt there, sweaty, flushed and panicking, and suddenly remembered a distant afternoon when he and his father had sat on the sitting-room floor and practised picking up change with a horseshoe magnet. If only he had a magnet now. Anything to spare him the humiliation that almost certainly lay ahead.

'Feel free to answer it, Dr Larenz,' shouted Anna.

The infernal ringing made it difficult to locate her voice, but Viktor guessed she was on the landing at the top of the stairs.

'Uh-huh,' he called back, unable to think of a more appropriate response. He could still see at least ten coins scattered over the floor and under the couch. One had made it as far as the fireplace, collided with the fender, and stopped.

'I don't mind if you answer it. I'm happy to wait.'

This time she sounded much closer. Viktor wondered what was keeping her. He glanced at the coins in his hand and froze. He had been chasing a stash of scrap metal. The contents of Anna's wallet consisted exclusively of Deutschmarks, which had been taken out of commission when the euro was introduced. Some people, Isabell included, liked to use the one-mark coins in supermarket trolleys, but Anna's collection numbered four dozen or more.

What was she doing with a wallet of obsolete coins? Surely everyone these days carried credit cards and ID?

*Who is she? How does she know about Josy? What's taking her so long?*

Viktor did the first thing that came into his head. Hastily, he shoved the half-empty wallet into Anna's pocket and bent down to sweep the remaining coins beneath the leather couch. There was no reason to think she would look there, and with any luck she wouldn't notice the missing marks.

He scanned the floor hurriedly and spotted a small slip of paper floating on the puddle of rainwater where Anna had hung her coat. It must have fallen out of the wallet with the coins. Viktor stooped down and pocketed it without thinking.

'Is something the matter?'

Straightening up, he came face to face with Anna. She must have crept into the room without him noticing. The odd thing was, he hadn't heard the door, even though the hinges creaked dreadfully.

'Oh, sorry, I was, um, I mean to say . . .'

In a dreadful moment of insight he realized how things would look from Anna's perspective. She had left the room for a few minutes and now here he was, sweaty and agitated, crawling around on the floor. There was nothing he could say.

'I hope it wasn't bad news?'

'I beg your pardon?'

And then it dawned on him why Anna had taken so long to come in.

He had been too busy worrying about the coins to realize that the phone had stopped ringing. Anna must have thought he had answered it and waited patiently in the hall.

'Oh, you mean the phone call,' he said, feeling stupid.

'Yes.'

'Wrong number.' He stood up shakily, only to jump a mile when the telephone rang again.

'That's persistence for you,' smiled Anna, taking a seat on the couch. 'Aren't you going to answer it?'

'Answer it? Err, yes ... Yes, of course,' stuttered Viktor, pulling himself together. 'I'll take the call in the kitchen. Excuse me one moment.'

Anna smiled serenely, and Viktor left the room.

As soon as he picked up the phone he realized that he had left something in the sitting room that would give him away. If Anna found it, she would know what he had done.

*The coin by the fender.*

He held the receiver to his ear and wondered how to regain her trust. As it happened, he didn't have long to worry about it. Just when he thought the situation couldn't possibly get any worse, he heard five words that eclipsed everything that had gone before.

# 21

'The blood was definitely female.'

'Female . . . What age?'

'I can't say,' replied Kai, his voice echoing strangely.

'Why not?'

'Because I'm not a geneticist.'

Viktor squeezed the back of his neck, but no amount of massaging could get rid of his headache.

'Where are you now?' he asked the PI.

'Westend Hospital. I know a guy who works in one of the labs. I had to sneak out into the corridor to call you because I'm not supposed to use my phone. They reckon it interferes with the equipment.'

'Standard hospital policy. You'd better be quick.'

'Here's the deal. This mate of mine is a biochemist. I talked him into running some tests in his lunch break. I gave him a phial of blood from your bathroom – although I probably could have given him a vat.'

'Just tell me the results.'

'Like I said, it came from a woman, older than nine and younger than fifty – but probably a whole lot younger than fifty.'

'Josy was twelve when she went missing.'

'It wasn't her blood.'

'How do you know?'

'It was fresh – a couple of days old; three at the outside. Josy has been missing for over four years.'

'I'm aware of that, thank you,' snapped Viktor, opening the kitchen door slightly and peering through the crack. The door to the sitting-room was closed, but he couldn't afford to take risks. He lowered his voice.

'Listen, if it's not Josy's blood, where does Anna fit into this? She described my daughter, she described the cabin in Sacrow, and she described our villa. She's not making it up. She was there, Kai. She knew all about Schwanenwerder. She even saw the reporters camped on the drive.'

'Anna? Is that her real name?'

'Yes.'

'Surname?'

Viktor took a deep breath, swallowed accidentally, and ended up coughing instead.

'Her name is . . .' He coughed again, holding the receiver at arm's length.

'Blasted flu. I'm sorry, Kai. Listen, I think I'd better tell you who she is. Her name is Anna Glass, she writes children's books, and she's pretty successful, especially in Japan. Her father worked for the American Forces Network and died from a botched appendicectomy when she was a kid. She grew up in Steglitz and was admitted to the Park four years ago. It's a private psychiatric clinic in Dahlem.'

The PI repeated the information and jotted down some notes. 'Fine, I'll check it out.'

'There's something else I'd like you to do for me.'

Viktor heard a long sigh on the other end of the line. 'What?'

'Have you still got the keys to the villa?'

'A digital card, right?'

'You swipe it to get through the gates.'

'Yep.'

'OK, I want you to go to my study and open the safe. You'll need to type in the code – Josy's date of birth backwards; year, month, then day. Inside you'll find a stack of CDs. You can't miss them.'

'And then what?'

'When Josy disappeared, the police asked me to save the footage from the security cameras.'

'Sure, they were hoping to spot the kidnapper in the crowd. They monitored the front of the house for a month.'

'I want you to find the disks for the first week and go through them.'

'Viktor, the footage has been examined tons of times. The police drew a blank.'

'They were looking for a man.'

'And you want me to look for a woman?'

'I want you to look for Anna: a small, slim blonde. Focus on the pack of reporters at the end of the drive. You've got her surname and other details. You should be able to find a photo on the web.'

There was a pause and when Kai finally responded, the line had improved. Viktor deduced that he was back in the lab.

1    'Fine,' the PI said reluctantly. 'If it makes you happy, I'll do it. But don't get your hopes up. Anna's stories, fascinating as they may be, are full of holes. True, there was a break-in in Sacrow, and true, there were reporters outside your house; but think of the time frame. It's four years out!'

'I know you think she's lying, but how else do you account for the blood? A little girl was murdered in my bathroom! If it wasn't Josy, who the hell was it?'

'Firstly, we don't know the age of the female in question, and secondly, no one was killed.'

'You said—'

'Listen to me, Viktor: no one was killed. In fact, the female was very definitely alive.'

'Alive?' he said, practically screaming into the phone. He was so exhausted and agitated that he had given up caring whether Anna was listening or not. 'She wouldn't have bled all over the bathroom if she were alive!'

'Viktor, you need to pay attention. There was mucus in the blood.'

'What difference does that—' He broke off and answered his own question. 'So she was . . .'

'Yes, and it's time you calmed down. The lab results were unambiguous. It was menstrual blood.'

# 22

## Room 1245, Berlin-Wedding Psychosomatic Clinic

It was dark outside. The clinic's automatic lighting had hummed into action and Dr Roth looked more anaemic than ever in the cold glare of the overhead lights. Viktor Larenz noticed for the first time that the consultant psychiatrist was balding at the temples. His stylishly cropped hair usually kept the telltale triangles well hidden, but for the past hour he had been raking his fingers nervously through his hair and ruining the effects of his grooming.

'You seem anxious, Dr Roth.'

'Not anxious, just curious about what happened next.'

Viktor requested a glass of water. His wrists were still strapped to the bed, so Roth had to hold the glass while he drank through a straw.

'There are a few things I'd like to ask,' said the psychiatrist as Viktor sipped thirstily.

'Go ahead.'

'Why didn't you make more of an effort to find Sindbad? If it was my dog, I'd be hunting high and low.'

'You're absolutely right. To be honest, I was surprised

by my own apathy. Looking back, I'd say I was emotionally and physically exhausted from searching for Josy. You know how veteran soldiers barely flinch when they hear a grenade? It was like I'd decided to stay in my trench and weather the next bombardment. Do you see what I mean?'

'Yes, but why didn't you tell your wife? Surely you must have thought to call her when the dog disappeared?'

'I did! I tried calling her almost every day, but I couldn't get through. I can't say I was looking forward to telling her about Anna. We'd already argued about the interview – unnecessarily, as it happens, because I was too distracted to work on it anyway. But if she'd known I was treating a patient . . .' He stopped and sighed. 'She would have taken the first plane home. In the end I didn't get the chance to speak to her because the receptionist wouldn't put me through. I had to content myself with leaving messages.'

'And she never called back?'

'She called once.'

'Were you able to clear things up?'

Rather than answering, Viktor signalled for more water. Dr Roth lifted the straw to his mouth.

'How long have I . . .' Viktor broke off, took a long sip and started again, 'Are we doing all right for time?'

'We've probably got another twenty minutes. Your lawyers have arrived. They're in Professor Malzius's office.'

*My lawyers.*

Viktor's last encounter with the legal profession dated back to 1997. The lawyer, a gawky fellow who specialized in traffic infringements, had successfully salvaged his licence; but only a real professional could help Viktor now. This time it wasn't about a ding in someone's car.

His future was at stake.

'The lawyers, are they any good?'

'Top-notch, I'm told. The best that money can buy.'

'I suppose they'll want to know what happened to Anna?'

'They'll be asking a lot of questions. How else are they supposed to construct a defence? You're being tried for murder, remember.'

There. He had finally said it: *murder*.

Neither of them had mentioned it explicitly, but the facts of the matter were plain: Viktor Larenz was heading for jail unless the conclusion of his story could convince the judge to throw out the case.

'I know what I'm being accused of, but I won't have the strength to go over the story again. Besides, I'm hoping to be out of here in twenty minutes.'

'No chance,' said Roth, putting down the glass of water. He ran a hand through his hair. 'Can we get on with the story? You were describing how Kai informed you about the blood. Did Anna have anything interesting to tell you when you got off the phone?'

'No.'

Dr Roth looked at him quizzically.

'She slipped out while I was talking to Kai. She left a

note on my desk, "Didn't want to interrupt. You're obviously busy. Will call round tomorrow." My nerves were in tatters, but with Anna gone, I had to resign myself to another night without knowing what happened.'

*Without knowing what became of Charlotte. And Josy.*

'So you went to bed?'

'Not exactly. That evening I had another unexpected visitor.'

# 23

Ten minutes after finishing his conversation with Kai, he heard a knock at the door. For a second he allowed himself to hope that Anna had returned. The disappointment was all the greater when it turned out to be none other than a grim-faced Halberstaedt on his second visit in the wind and rain. Once again he declined Viktor's invitation to come inside and handed him a package.

'What is it?'

'A pistol.'

Viktor recoiled as if Halberstaedt had confessed to harbouring some kind of infectious disease.

'What on earth would I want with a pistol?'

'It's so you can defend yourself.'

'From what?'

'From her.' Halberstaedt jabbed a thumb in the direction of the beach. 'I saw her leave.'

Viktor could scarcely believe his ears. He fished a tissue out of his pocket and dabbed at his nose without actually blowing it. 'Listen Patrick, I've always respected your opinions, but I can't allow you to harass my patients. As her therapist, it's my duty to protect her.'

'And as the mayor, it's my duty to protect you.'

'Thank you, Patrick, I appreciate your concern, but I've no intention of keeping it.' He tried to return the gun, but Halberstaedt kept his hands in the pockets of his threadbare cords. 'Besides,' said Viktor, 'you can't go round making serious allegations without any proof.'

'Who says I haven't?'

'Haven't what?'

'Got proof,' replied Halberstaedt grimly. 'Keep the weapon; you might need it. I've been watching that woman and asking around.'

'Oh really?' There was a metallic taste in Viktor's mouth. He thought of Kai Strathmann; there were at least two people on Anna's trail.

'She gave Burg a hell of a shock, you know.'

'The ferryman? I didn't think Michael Burg was the type to be frightened by a woman.'

'She's got unfinished business with you, that's what she said.'

'Unfinished business?'

'She said something about letting some blood.'

'That's preposterous!'

*A bathroom full of blood.*

Halberstaedt shrugged. 'I'm only telling you what Burg told me. Look, it's fine if you don't believe me, but do me a favour and keep the gun. I'm worried about that carving knife.'

Viktor didn't know what to say. He suddenly remembered a completely separate but equally urgent problem.

Halberstaedt turned to leave, but Viktor tapped him

on the back. 'I was meaning to ask you something. Have you seen my dog?'

'Is Sindbad dead?'

Viktor was stunned by his brutal directness. It was like surviving an earthquake, only to be hit by the after-shock. And he couldn't help feeling that the biggest blow was yet to come.

'Dead? What makes you think ... I mean, no, or at least, I hope not. He's gone missing. I left a message on your answerphone.'

'Uh-huh,' muttered Halberstaedt, inclining his head. 'I told you there was something funny about that woman.'

Viktor wondered whether to point out that Anna had nothing to do with Sindbad's disappearance, but he decided not to bother.

'I'll let you know if I see him,' promised Halberstaedt. He didn't seem particularly concerned.

'Thank you.'

'Look after yourself, Dr Larenz. That woman is dangerous.'

The mayor left without another word.

Viktor gazed after him for a while, then realized that it was freezing outside. He felt like a small boy who had stayed in the pool until his hands went blue. He closed the door hastily before the wind filled the house with cold wet air.

Halfway along the hall, he stopped and considered. Maybe he should throw the pistol in the outside bin? He felt nervous around weapons and the very idea of having a gun in the house was somehow alarming. In the end he resolved to take it back to Halberstaedt in the morning. For the time being, he placed the unopened package in the bottom drawer of the mahogany bureau by the door.

Viktor spent the next few minutes staring into the dying embers of the hearth and trying to make sense of the day's events.

Sindbad had vanished.

A woman or maybe a girl had broken into his cabin in Sacrow and left menstrual blood in the bathroom.

And the mayor of Parkum had knocked on his door and handed him a gun.

Viktor took off his shoes and lay down on the couch. Fumbling in his pocket, he took out his last remaining Valium tablet, decided not to save it for later as intended, and waited for the sedative to kick in. As much as anything, he needed something to ease the effects of his flu. Closing his eyes, he focused on eradicating the pain that was holding his head in a vice. It worked for a short while and for the first time in ages he was able to breathe through one side of his nose. The heavy aroma of Anna's perfume was still potent in the air, thirty minutes after she had got up from the couch.

Viktor's mind was churning. He wasn't sure what was more worrying: Anna's erratic behaviour or the mayor's sinister warnings.

He didn't reach a satisfactory conclusion because a moment later the nightmare began.

# 24

It had been haunting him since Josy's disappearance, sometimes three times a week, sometimes once a month; there was no fixed pattern to when it happened, but the chain of events was always the same.

When the nightmare started, Viktor was always at the wheel of his Volvo with Josy in the passenger seat. It was the middle of the night and they were driving to see a specialist who had recently opened a practice on the North German seaboard. The journey had taken hours already and Viktor was driving too fast, but the Volvo was stuck in fifth gear. From time to time Josy begged him to slow down, but the car was setting the pace. Considering their speed, it was lucky that the road was dead straight: no corners, no turn-offs, no traffic lights, no junctions. Periodically, another vehicle would hurtle towards them, but they were never in danger of colliding because the lanes were generously sized. After a while Viktor remarked on the length of the journey. Josy shrugged, apparently as baffled as he was. By rights, they should have reached the coast ages ago, especially since they were eating up the kilometres at an incredible rate. The road seemed oddly deserted, and stranger still, it was getting darker all the time. In fact, the streetlights were getting fewer and further between and the trees were closing in. After a while they were driving in total darkness, with dense woodland on either side of the narrowing road.

This was the point at which he started to feel uneasy – not panicked or frightened, but vaguely apprehensive. His sense of dread deepened when he discovered that the car wouldn't stop. He stamped on the brakes but nothing happened. A moment later, the Volvo picked up speed, accelerating down the endless stretch of linear tarmac. Switching on the reading light, he told Josy to find out where they were, but the map didn't help.

At last she pointed ahead and laughed in relief.

'Look, there's a light. We must be nearly there.'

Viktor made out a faint glow in the distance. The light became brighter as they approached.

'Keep going straight on,' said Josy. 'It looks like a village – or maybe the lights of the coast road.'

Viktor nodded, his heart slowing to something like its normal rate. It was reassuring to think they would soon be there. They sped up again, this time because he was flooring the car. He couldn't wait to reach the coast, to leave the forest and darkness behind him.

In an instant the feeling was back.

His stomach started to knot.

Everything was terrifyingly clear. True, there was a light ahead, but Josy had mistaken its purpose. And he too had been mistaken, mistaken to think that their journey through the darkness could come to any good. Josy had noticed what was up and was staring out of her passenger window in terror.

The road wasn't lined with trees; there was nothing on either side of them but water. Deep, cold, fathomless water.

The realization came too late. Viktor knew there was nothing he could do.

They were driving down a pier. All the while they had been looking for the coast, but the beach was kilometres behind them and the car was racing out to sea, hurtling towards the beacon, and there was nothing he could do.

He tried spinning the wheel, but it was jammed. Viktor wasn't driving the Volvo; the Volvo was driving him.

They covered the last few metres at breakneck speed, the pier ran out, the car launched itself into the air, soaring above the sinister waves of the cold North Sea. The bonnet started to dip and Viktor peered through the windscreen, hoping to catch a glimpse of something in the glow of the headlights. But all he could see was the deep, dark water that was about to swallow them: Josy, the Volvo and himself.

He always woke in the split second before the car splashed down. It was the climax of the nightmare, not only because he knew that he and his daughter were destined to drown, but because he was dumb enough to glance in the rear-view mirror as they sped towards the waves. And as he stared at the mirror, he screamed at the top of his voice, yanking himself out of the nightmare and waking Isabell if she was in the room. What he saw in the rear-view mirror was the apogee of horror. He saw nothing. The mirror was blank.

The pier that jutted into the sea for kilometres, the pier whose beacon they had been racing towards at lightning speed, was gone. It had vanished into thin air.

# 25

Viktor sat up with a jolt and realized that his pyjamas were drenched in sweat. The sheet was soaking as well and his sore throat had definitely worsened in the course of his nightmare.

*What's the matter with me?* he wondered, waiting for his heart to settle. At some point before falling asleep he must have got up from the couch and made his way to bed, but he couldn't remember going upstairs, let alone getting undressed. And that wasn't the only thing that was bothering him. The bedroom was really cold. He reached out with his right hand, fumbling in the darkness for the battery-operated alarm clock on his bedside table. At the press of a button, the display lit up, showing the time and temperature: half past three in the morning and only eight degrees, from which he concluded that the generator had cut out. He flicked the switch on his bedside lamp to test the theory. The power was down.

He cursed his misfortune. First the flu, then Anna's strange stories, Sindbad's disappearance, his nightmare and now this. He threw off the covers and lumbered to his feet, remembering to pick up the mini Maglite that he kept by his bed for precisely this reason. Shivering, he crept down the creaking stairs, his torch beam roving over the photographs on the wall. Under normal circumstances, he wasn't easily frightened, but there was something eerie about what he saw: his mother, laughing, on the beach with the dogs; his father smoking a pipe by the fire; the whole family admiring his father's catch.

The images flared up like memories in the first stages of anaesthesia, dazzling him for a moment, then fading into the void.

As Viktor opened the door, he was hit by a ferocious gust of wind that blew the last of the autumn leaves and a flurry of raindrops into the house. *Bloody marvellous. I'll be laid up with pneumonia at this rate.*

Still in his silk pyjamas, he put on his trainers and pulled a blue cagoule over his head. The shed was only twenty or so metres from the door. Hood up, he scurried along the waterlogged path. His torch wasn't powerful enough to light up the potholes left by the rain, and he had barely covered half the distance before his feet and calves were drenched. Water was lashing against his face, but he couldn't walk any faster in case he tripped up. His first-aid kit, already depleted because of his cold, contained nothing that would help with twisted ankles or fractured bones. It was pitch-black, he was kilometres from the village, and the island was cut off from civilization by the storm: a broken leg was probably the last thing he needed.

At last he was almost at his goal, a corrugated-iron

shed on the edge of his land, bordering the public beach. It was closed off by a dilapidated white fence.

Viktor had vivid memories of weatherproofing the fence. At his father's insistence, he had helped with every step of the arduous ritual, which started with sanding and staining the wood and finished with the application of an exceptionally foul-smelling paint. The wood had been slightly rotten even then, but after years of neglect, the fence and the generator were in similar states of disrepair. With any luck, the generator could still be fixed.

He brushed the water out of his eyes and came to a sudden halt. *Botheration.* Even as he reached for the cracked plastic handle he knew it was no good. The door was locked and the key was hanging by the fuse box in the basement. He would have to go back. *Damn!*

Viktor aimed a kick at the door and nearly jumped out of his skin. The corrugated iron made a terrible racket. 'Oh well,' he mumbled, 'at least I don't have to worry about the neighbours. And in this weather I don't suppose anyone will be out for a stroll.'

He was talking out loud and sweating profusely in spite of the cold. He threw back his hood. And then a strange thing happened; the world slowed down. It felt to Viktor as if someone had stopped his inner clock. He was caught in a split second that lasted an eternity. Everything unfolded incredibly slowly in his mind.

Three things surfaced in his consciousness. The first was a noise that had come to his attention as soon as he slipped back his hood. The generator was humming. *Why would it hum if it's broken?*

The second was a light. Viktor looked up at the house and saw that a light had come on in his room. The lamp on his bedside table was producing a soft yellow glow.

The third was a person. There was someone in his bedroom. And that someone was looking out of the window, looking at him.

*Anna?*

Viktor set off at a run, dropping his torch. He realized his error when the bedroom light went out before he reached the porch. The house and the garden were plunged into darkness, obliging him to retrace his steps and go back for the torch. He picked it up, hurried to the porch and entered the hall. Charging up the stairs with his fading torch, he saw the ghostly faces in the darkness. He stormed into his bedroom. Nothing.

Panting with exertion, he shone the beam in all four corners of the room: teak furniture by the window, an antique chest of drawers and beside it Isabell's dressing table, where he had dumped a stack of CDs, then the imposing sight of his parents' marital bed. There was no sign of anyone, not even when Viktor switched on the lights. The generator was clearly working again.

*Had it been working all along?*

Viktor sat on the bed. He needed to catch his breath and gather his thoughts. *Anna, Josy, Sindbad.* He wondered whether he was suffering from stress. What had possessed him to leave the house at half past three in the morning to fix a generator that was obviously working? He should have been tucked up in bed, convalescing, instead of chasing phantom apparitions through the wind and rain.

He got up, made his way round the bed and picked up his alarm clock: 20.5° Celsius. *Unbelievable.* The temperature was back to normal.

He shook his head. *In that case it must be me.*

He went downstairs to close the door.

*You had a horrible nightmare*, he comforted himself. *What do you expect? And you're under a lot of stress, what with Sindbad disappearing and your flu getting worse.* He bolted the door, only to undo it a moment later. Stooping down, he fished out the spare key from under the flowerpot. *You can't be too careful*, he told himself. After checking the ground-floor windows, he started to feel more himself.

As soon as he was in bed, he took a long draught of cough mixture and spent the next few hours dozing fitfully.

The wind that night was determined to live up to the weather forecaster's predictions and battered Parkum with heavy gusts and driving rain. It whipped the North Sea into towering waves and hurled them at the little island with primeval force, then rushed up the beach with undiminished fury. The hurricane snapped branches, rattled windows and erased all signs of activity from the sand. It also obliterated the delicate trail of footprints leading away from Viktor Larenz's house.

# 26

## *The day before the truth, Parkum*

Shortly after eight o'clock Viktor was woken by the phone. Wearily, he dragged himself downstairs and picked up the receiver, hoping to hear his wife. But it wasn't Isabell returning his calls.

'Did you find my note?'

*Anna.*

'Yes.' Viktor tried to clear his throat and ended up coughing. Anna had to wait a few seconds for him to recover.

'After yesterday's session I couldn't stop thinking about Charlotte. I thought about coming back, but I didn't want to disturb you.'

*Uh-huh, so you waited outside and broke into my room?*

'I'm ready to tell you the end of the story.'

*The end of Josy's story.*

'That's excellent progress,' croaked Viktor, wondering why Anna hadn't remarked on his wretched state of health. It was probably because she sounded pretty lousy herself, although it was hard to tell with the crackling on the line. She was only a few kilometres away, but the sound quality was terrible. It reminded him of the frustrations of inter-national calling before the technology improved.

'Could I tell you the rest on the phone? I don't feel up to visiting, but I'd like to get it off my chest.'

'No problem.'

Viktor glanced irritably at his bare feet. He had for-gotten to put on his slippers or dressing gown.

'If I remember rightly, I was explaining how Charlotte and I left the palace.'

'That's right. You said you were being chased.'

Viktor used his foot to manoeuvre a small Persian rug from under the table. At least he wouldn't have to stand bare-footed on the floor anymore.

'I took Charlotte by the hand, ran to the car, and drove off. Charlotte wanted to go to Hamburg but she wouldn't say why. I gave up and let her dictate the route.'

'What happened when you got there?'

'We checked in to the Hyatt on Mönckebergstrasse. Charlotte didn't care where we stayed, so I went for the Park Hyatt because I wanted a bit of luxury and it reminded me of my days as a glamorous author. I used to meet my agent in the lobby, and I always thought the hotel had an exalted feel to it. I was hoping it would help me focus on happier times.'

Viktor nodded. At one time in his life he had regularly stayed in the five-star Hyatt, preferably on the executive floor.

'Unfortunately it had the opposite effect. I felt irritable and depressed. I couldn't think clearly and Charlotte was becoming a handful. The poor thing was suffering, and she put the blame on me. I gave her some paracetamol and a dose of penicillin, and thankfully she fell asleep. I was desperate to get on with the book.'

'The book about Charlotte?'

'Yes. I wanted to put an end to the nightmare and the only solution was to finish the book – at least, that was my rationale. After a lot of thought, I realized how to handle the story.'

'How?'

'Charlotte's clues were the key to the story. I had to describe the cause of her illness based on what I'd seen. The first clue was the cabin in the forest; that was the beginning, according to her. I decided to write a chapter where she goes to the cabin and falls ill.'

*Josy fell ill in Schwanenwerder, not Sacrow,* thought Viktor. *It started on Boxing Day. We had to call the doctor.*

'Then I realized that Charlotte had been referring to something else. I remembered how she had told me to "look for what's missing".'

*Her dressing table? A television? A poster of Eminem?*

'At last I understood what she meant: she was asking me to look for *changes*. Something dreadful had happened in that cabin, something so terrible that she had never set foot in there again. I realized that it had to be associated with the person behind the door.'

There was a long pause while Viktor waited for her to continue.

'Well?' he said at last.

'Well what?'

*Why does she have to be so obtuse?* To Viktor's credit, he bit his tongue. He was tired of coaxing the information out of her, but he didn't want to upset her in case she broke off the story at the critical point.

'How did you finish the story?'

'Haven't you guessed? I should have thought it was obvious.'

'In what way?'

'Come on, Dr Larenz, you're the analyst. I think you can work it out.'

'It's your story, not mine.'

'You're beginning to sound like Charlotte,' she said brightly.

Viktor wasn't in the mood for playing games. He was waiting for an answer.

Four years he had waited for an answer. Four years of fearing the answer, fearing and looking. A thousand scenarios had been enacted in his mind. And while his daughter had died a thousand imaginary deaths, he had died a thousand times at her side. He was dead, and nothing could hurt him – or so he thought. But when Anna finally spoke, he realized that he was vulnerable after all. 'She was poisoned,' she explained.

No amount of warning could have prepared him for that. Viktor took fast, shallow breaths. He was suddenly grateful for the numbing cold in the sitting room for without it the shock would surely be worse. He had an urge to throw up, but he didn't have the strength to run upstairs.

'Dr Larenz?'

He knew she was expecting a response, and he tried to think what he would say if he were just her therapist and not the grief-stricken father of her delusions. Officially, Charlotte was a hallucination, the result of faulty wiring in Anna's brain.

To buy himself some time, he used the psychiatrist's stock comeback: 'Tell me more.'

It was another fatal mistake. Anna's first revelation was nothing compared to what came next.

# 27

'Poisoned?' boomed Kai in a voice that, even by his standards, was unnaturally loud. He had just left Schwanenwerder and was on his way back to the office in central Berlin. 'Why does the Glass woman think the kid was poisoned?'

'No idea. I guess she came up with a story that fitted the facts.'

'Facts? What facts? She's a mental patient!'

Viktor heard frantic tooting, from which he deduced that Kai, who couldn't be bothered with a hands-free kit, was negotiating the motorway one-handed again. 'Anna thinks something happened in Sacrow. According to her, Josy—'

'You mean, Charlotte,' Kai corrected him.

'That's what I said, didn't I? But let's imagine she was talking about Josy. According to Anna, something dreadful happened in the cabin, something that shook the foundations of her world. That was the trigger.'

'The trigger for what? For someone to poison her?'

'Precisely.'

'And who the hell is supposed to have poisoned her?'

'Josy.'

'Excuse me?'

The roar of traffic faded abruptly. Kai must have pulled into the hard shoulder and stopped.

'Josy poisoned herself. That was the crux of Anna's story. Josy was so distressed by whatever happened in the cabin that she decided to take her own life. She did it gradually and in small doses so that the doctors wouldn't know.'

'Steady on, Viktor. What are you trying to say?'

'I don't expect you to be an expert on psychiatry, but maybe you've heard of Munchausen syndrome?'

'Hmm, Munchausen, isn't that a fancy name for pathological lying?'

'Sort of. People suffering from Munchausen's make themselves unwell because they want to be noticed. They realize that they get more attention when they're ill.'

'You mean they'd poison themselves to get a few visitors?'

'They want people to feel sorry for them. It's nice to get grapes and chocolates and other presents. Munchausen patients crave sympathy.'

'That's loopy.'

'It's a serious condition, and Munchausen patients are often excellent actors, which makes it difficult to diagnose. I've seen cases where sufferers have simulated medical problems so convincingly that experienced doctors have fallen for the act. Treatment is given for the phantom symptoms while the underlying illness – the Munchausen's – is ignored. Of course, some patients are able to induce genuine physical symptoms, for instance by ingesting weed killer and presenting with an ulcer.'

'Hang on a minute ... You don't think your own daughter ... I mean, Josy was only eleven when she had her first attack!'

'And perhaps it was poison that induced it, who knows? To be honest, Kai, I'm tired of not knowing. I feel like part of my life is shrouded in darkness, and I need to shed light on it. I know Anna's delusional, but I can't help wondering if she's right. It might be unlikely, but it's certainly not impossible. I'd rather have a more comforting explanation, but it's the only one we've got.'

'OK, let's pretend for a moment that you're not completely crazy.' Judging by the noise in the background, Kai had left the hard shoulder and rejoined the flow of traffic. 'Suppose Anna is right and Josy poisoned herself, there's one blindingly obvious question: *how*? Don't try to convince me that a little kid would know enough about drugs to pick one that would poison her so slowly that the best doctors in the country would be fooled.'

'I didn't say I had the answer, Kai. Look, maybe parts of Anna's story don't make sense, maybe none of it hangs together. All I care about is whether any of this has a bearing on Josy. It's why I put you on the case.'

'Fine, I'll look into it. I was going to call you anyway. I just made the weirdest discovery.'

'What?' Sweat was running down Viktor's back. He wasn't sure whether to put it down to panic or the flu.

'I followed your instructions. I went to your house to get the disks from the safe. Are you sitting down?'

'Don't tell me the disks weren't there.'

'No, but the footage from the first week has been wiped.'

'Wiped? The disks were write-protected. You'd have to destroy them to get rid of the data.'

'Well someone has managed it. I fetched the disks as soon as we got off the phone and went through them this morning. They're blank.'

'All of them?'

'No, just the disks from the first week. That's what's so weird. I thought maybe you'd got the cases mixed up and put the disks somewhere else, so I went back to check. The first week's footage is gone.'

Viktor could feel himself swaying and clung to the mantelpiece. 'What do you think of my theory now?' he asked the PI. 'I suppose you still think it's a coincidence and Anna made everything up?'

'No, but . . .'

'Come on, Kai, this is our first real lead in four years. I'll be damned if I'm letting you dismiss it.'

'I'm not dismissing anything. I'm just worried about Anna Glass.'

'What about her?'

'There's something funny about her.'

'She's schizophrenic.'

'Apart from that. I checked her out. We cross-referenced every single fact.'

'What did you find?'

'Nothing.'

'Nothing?'

'We found nothing at all.'

'That's good, isn't it?'

'It's bloody alarming. It means she doesn't exist.'

'I don't follow.'

'Anna Glass doesn't exist. We couldn't find any authors by that name, let alone bestselling authors with fan clubs in Japan. She didn't grow up in Berlin, she didn't have a father who worked for the AFN, and she never lived in Steglitz.'

'Damn. Have you checked with the Park?'

'They're still stalling. It's a classy place, but not so classy that I won't find someone who'll spill the details in return for some cash. I thought the guy who took over from you at the clinic might be able to help – Professor van Druisen.'

'No.'

'What's the big deal?'

'I'd rather handle it myself. In this instance, I'll be able to get my hands on the information faster than you. Let me tackle the clinic and van Druisen. See what else you can find and take another look at Josy's room. We left it exactly the way it was. You might spot something new.'

*Pills? Chemicals?*

There was no need for Viktor to spell it out.

'OK.'

'And find out whether anyone can remember a blonde woman and a sick little girl checking into the Park Hyatt in Hamburg four years ago.'

'Why?'

'Just do it.'

'It was four years ago, Viktor! I doubt anyone at the Hyatt has worked there that long.'

'Please, Kai.'

'Fine, but you've got to promise me something.'

'What?'

'Stay away from Anna Glass. Don't let her into the house. I don't want her near you until we know who she is. She might be dangerous.'

'We'll see.'

'I mean it, Viktor. I won't keep my side of the bargain unless you cut off all contact with that woman. You've got to be careful.'

'I'll do my best.'

Viktor hung up the phone. Kai's voice was still echoing in his head.

*Be careful. She might be dangerous.*

He had been given the same advice by two people in twenty-four hours. He was beginning to think they might be right.

# 28

'Park Clinic, Dahlem. Karin Vogt speaking. How can I help?'

'Hello, this is Viktor Larenz, *Dr* Viktor Larenz. A patient of mine spent a number of years in your care. I'd like to speak to the consulting doctor, if I may.'

'Certainly, Dr Larenz,' trilled Karin. 'If you could tell me his name . . .'

'That's the problem. I don't know the name of the doctor, but I can give you the patient's name.'

'In that case, I can't help you. Patient records are strictly confidential, as I'm sure you're aware. I'd be breaching our code of conduct if I gave out that kind of information. The simplest solution would be to ask your patient and then call back.'

'I'm afraid it's not possible.' *First, I don't know where she is. Second, I don't want her to know that I'm suspicious. And third, I need to find out what she did to my daughter.* 'She's not in a position to tell me.'

'Can't you look in her notes?' asked Karin, who was in danger of losing her trill.

'It wasn't an official referral. She came to see me of her own accord. Look, I applaud you for respecting the privacy of your patients. You obviously do a great job, and I don't want to waste your time, but if you could do me one small favour, I'll leave you in peace. It's just a matter of looking up a name on your computer. If you find it, you can transfer me to the consultant in charge of the appropriate unit. That way you're helping me and my patient without breaching your code.'

Viktor could practically see her tossing her glossy hair indecisively while she made up her mind.

'Please, Ms Vogt,' he said, smiling as he spoke. His friendly manner did the trick. Viktor could hear her tapping away at her computer.

'What's her name?'

'Glass,' he said quickly. 'Anna Glass.'

The tapping stopped abruptly. 'Is this your idea of a joke?' she demanded. The trill had definitely gone.

'A joke?'

'Any other "patients" you'd like me to check for? Elvis Presley, perhaps?'

'I'm afraid I don't follow . . .'

'Listen to me, Dr Larenz . . .' Karin Vogt sighed angrily. 'If this is some kind of hoax, you've got a sick sense of humour. And don't even think of recording this conversation – I know my rights.'

Viktor had no idea what to make of her sudden change of heart, but he wasn't going to take it lying down. 'No, Ms Vogt, you listen to me. My name is Dr Viktor Larenz, and I'm not in the business of making spoof calls. If you don't give me a sensible answer in the next thirty seconds, I'll inform Professor Malzius that his receptionist is extremely rude. He and I are golfing associates, you should know.'

It was a double lie: Viktor found Professor Malzius almost as abhorrent as playing golf. But it worked.

'I'm sorry I snapped, Dr Larenz. I found your question upsetting.'

'Upsetting? I thought you'd agreed to check my patient's name?'

'Dr Larenz, I was the one who found her. Surely you must have read the reports?'

*Found her?*

'Found her where?'

'On the floor. It was dreadful, really dreadful . . . Now, if you don't mind, Dr Larenz, I have to answer another call. I've got three people on hold.'

'I'm sorry, what was so dreadful about it?' asked Viktor, trying to make sense of what he had heard.

'She drowned in her own blood. Isn't that dreadful enough?'

*Dead? Anna is dead? But it doesn't . . .*

'I'm afraid I don't follow. I saw her yesterday.'

'Yesterday? There must be some mistake. I found Anna's body in the ward office a year ago. There was nothing I could do.'

*A year ago?*

'How did a patient get into the ward office?' wondered Viktor. He had been pondering a hundred different questions, but this one came out first.

'Dr Larenz, it's hard to believe that you don't know what happened, but I'll tell you all the same. Anna Glass wasn't a patient; she was a student on an internship. She's dead, I'm still here, and I have to get on. All right?'

'Yes.'

*No, not really, it's not all right at all.*

'One last thing. What happened? How did she die?'

'She was poisoned. Anna Glass was poisoned.'

Viktor dropped the receiver and stared out of the window. Nothing but darkness, impenetrable darkness.

Like the darkness overhead.

# 29

Later, when he developed nausea, diarrhoea and blurred vision, he could no longer ignore the evidence that he had contracted something more serious than a cold. None of his usual remedies – aspirin, vitamin C, and throat spray – seemed to be having much effect. And his beloved Assam tea, far from soothing his sore throat, was actually making it worse. In fact, the bitter aftertaste was getting stronger with every cup, leading him to wonder if he had forgotten to strain the pot.

The beginning of the end coincided with Anna's penultimate visit to the house. She turned up unannounced that afternoon while he was napping fitfully. Still wearing his pyjamas and dressing gown, he dragged himself to the door.

'Are you still feeling poorly?' she enquired straightaway.

He wondered how long she had been knocking. In his dream, a pneumatic drill had been going for some time before he realized that it was someone at the door.

'I'm just a bit under the weather. I thought we arranged to talk this evening?'

'We did. Don't worry, I won't disturb you. I just dropped by to give you this.'

On seeing that she was holding something, he opened the door a little further and was shocked to see that Anna looked a mess. There was almost nothing left of the smart, attractive young woman who had appeared in his sitting room four days earlier. She hadn't brushed her hair, and her blouse looked creased. Her eyes were flicking nervously back and forth while she drummed her long slim fingers on a brown manila envelope that she was clutching with both hands.

'What's that?'

'The end of the book – the final ten chapters describing everything I went through with Charlotte. It was playing on my mind, so I decided to write the story again from memory.'

*When? At half past three in the morning, after breaking into my house? Or four hours later, when you called me at home?*

She ran a hand over the envelope, smoothing the package lovingly as if it were a gift.

Viktor hesitated. His good sense advised him not to let Anna into the house.

*She's dangerous.*

The evidence so far was damning: Anna Glass wasn't who she claimed to be. He knew for a fact that her name belonged to a student who had been poisoned at the Park. But this woman, whoever she was, held the key to Josy's disappearance. If he didn't seize his chance, he might never answer the questions that were driving him to distraction.

And since he was desperate to know who she was and why she thought they had 'unfinished business', he decided to ask her whatever he wanted. It didn't matter anymore if she clammed up or stormed out because she had already given him the final chapters of Charlotte's story.

'Wait,' he said quickly, opening the door fully. 'Why don't you come in for a moment? You must be frozen out there.'

'Thanks.' Anna shook the rain out of her long blonde hair and stepped nervously into the warmth.

He ushered her into the sitting room while he lingered in the hall. As soon as he was alone, he opened the bottom drawer of the bureau, took out Halberstaedt's package and ran his fingers over the crumpled paper. The string fell away as the knot came free.

'Could I possibly have a cup of tea?'

Viktor stood up sharply and dropped the half-opened package. Anna was standing in the corridor. She had taken off her coat and was wearing black trousers with a sheer slate-grey blouse that was buttoned all wrong.

'Of course,' he said, taking a handkerchief out of the drawer and closing it quickly. As far as he could tell, she hadn't noticed what was in the parcel.

After steering her back into the sitting room, he hurried to the kitchen and reappeared a few minutes later with the tea. He was feeling so drained that carrying a full pot seemed downright impossible, so he had only filled it halfway.

'Thank you.'

Anna barely seemed to notice him and didn't appear in the least surprised when he stopped to mop the sweat from his brow before stumbling to his desk.

'I should probably get going,' she said as soon as he sat down.

'But you haven't touched your tea!'

He slipped the first sheet out of the envelope and read the title: *The Passage*.

To his surprise, it was a laser-printed manuscript. She had obviously brought her laptop with her and talked Trudi, the proprietor of the Anchor, into letting her use the printer in the office.

'Please, Dr Larenz, I really can't stay.'

'OK, I'll read the manuscript later,' he said, shoving the page clumsily into the envelope. 'But while you're here, I'd like to ask you about last night. What—' He looked up at Anna and stopped short.

There was definitely something the matter. Anna's eyes were fixed nervously on the ceiling and she was clenching her fists. Whatever was raging inside her seemed determined to get out. He desperately wanted to know whether she had broken into his house and why she had lied about her name, but he knew it would be irresponsible to bother her in her present state. No matter how much he wanted some answers, there could be no justification for precipitating a psychotic episode in a patient who needed his help. At last he decided to tackle the reason she had come to him in the first place: her schizophrenia.

'How long have you got?' he asked gently.

'Till the next episode?'

'Yes.'

'A day? Twelve hours? I don't know. The symptoms are there already,' she said in a strained voice.

'Colours?'

'Yes, everything around me is brighter, more intense. It looks as if someone has varnished the trees and turned the sea a deep, shiny blue. I can hardly bear to look away; it's so incredibly radiant, even in the rain. And the smell is fabulous too. I can smell the salt in the air. It's like everything is steeped in the most wonderful perfume and no one can smell it except me.'

It was roughly what Viktor had expected her to say, but it was sobering all the same. He couldn't say for sure whether Anna was dangerous, but she was definitely ill. And dealing with a schizophrenic patient in the grip of a delusion was no joke – especially on an island in the middle of nowhere.

'Any voices?'

Anna shook her head. 'No, but it's only a matter of time. I'm a textbook schizophrenic: heightened colours, imaginary voices, then the visual hallucinations. At least I won't have to worry about seeing Charlotte this time.'

'Why not?'

'Because Charlotte won't be coming back. She's gone for good.'

'How can you be so sure?'

'You'll know if you read the manuscript. I—'

Viktor wasn't able to hear the rest because the telephone rang and Anna fell silent.

'What happened to Charlotte?' he persisted.

'You should answer the phone, Dr Larenz. I've resigned myself to it ringing while I'm here. Besides, I wasn't intending to stay.'

'I can't let you go. You're on the brink of another episode; you need help.'

*And I need some answers. What happened to Charlotte?*

'Stay right here,' he instructed her. Anna stared at the floor, rubbing her index finger nervously against her thumbnail. Viktor noticed that the cuticle was red raw. She obviously had a nervous tick.

'Fine, I'll stay for a bit,' she agreed. 'But stop that awful ringing.'

# 30

He answered the phone in the kitchen.

'I was beginning to think you were out,' said Kai impatiently. 'You're never going to believe what happened.'

'Hang on a second,' whispered Viktor, placing the receiver on the work surface next to the sink. He pulled off his slippers and crept, barefoot, into the hall, talking loudly as if he were on the phone.

'Yes ... Really? ... All right ... Leave it to me.'

Peering into the sitting room, he was relieved to see that Anna was sitting exactly where he had left her.

'OK, we can talk,' he said when he was back in the kitchen.

'She's not there, is she?'

'Yes.'

'I thought we had an agreement.'

'She turned up on the doorstep, and I couldn't exactly turn her away. It's not safe to be outside in this weather. Anyway, I thought you wanted to tell me something?'

'A fax arrived at the office today.'

'Who from?'

'I don't know. I'd like you to take a look at it.'

'What does it say?'

'Nothing.'

'You're ringing to tell me that you received a blank fax?'

'I didn't say it was blank. There's no message; just a picture.'

'A picture? What's it got to do with me?'

'I think it's from your daughter. I think Josy drew it.'

Trembling, Viktor leant back against the fridge and closed his eyes.

'When?'

'When what?'

'When did you get the fax?'

'About an hour ago. It was sent directly to me. Only a handful of people know my private number.'

Viktor took a deep breath and ended up coughing again. 'I don't know what to make of it.'

'Do you have a fax machine at your end?'

'It's on the desk in the sitting room.'

'Great. I'll fax it through in ten minutes. In the meantime, get that woman out of the house. I'll call back in a bit so you can tell me what you think.'

Viktor reeled off his fax number and hung up.

As soon as he was in the hall, he saw that the door to the sitting room was closed. Cursing inwardly, he immediately suspected that Anna had done another disappearing act. He yanked the door open and heaved a sigh of relief. Anna was still there. She was standing at the desk with her back to him.

'Hello again,' he said in a voice so hoarse that it was barely a whisper.

His relief gave way to horror. Anna hadn't heard him come in: she still had her back to him and was stirring white powder into his tea.

# 31

'Get out of my house!'

Anna turned round slowly and looked at him blankly.

'Goodness me, Doctor, you nearly gave me a heart attack. Is something wrong?'

'Wrong? My tea has tasted bitter for days, I've been feeling wretched ever since you came to the island, and now I know why!'

'For heaven's sake, Dr Larenz, you're going to make yourself ill. Calm down and take a seat.'

'Of course I'm ill! You've been spiking my tea with . . . Well, you tell me!'

'I beg your pardon?'

'What the hell have you been putting in my tea?' bellowed Viktor. The words seemed to scrape against the inside of his throat, making his voice quiver hysterically.

'Pull yourself together,' she said briskly.

'WHAT'S IN MY TEA?'

'Paracetamol.'

'Paracetamol?'

'Yes, it's great for colds.' She opened her grey designer handbag. 'See for yourself. I had such an ordeal with Charlotte that I never leave home without it.' She paused. 'You looked so awful that I wanted to help. I was going to tell you before you drank it, but then . . . Oh heavens, you didn't think I was trying to poison you, did you?'

Viktor was thinking all sorts of things, but he didn't know what to believe.

His dog had disappeared, and he himself was suffering from diarrhoea, a temperature and myalgia – classic symptoms of a viral infection. *Or poison.* Cough medicine and painkillers didn't seem to help.

And two people had warned him independently about Anna.

*Be careful; she's dangerous.*

'Look,' said Anna, showing him her cup. 'I put paracetamol in mine as well. I thought it might do us some good. I'd hardly want to poison myself, would I? I've drunk a few sips already.'

Viktor stared at her, aghast. He was still too agitated to find the right words. 'What am I supposed to think?' he shouted. 'None of it makes any sense! Why the hell would you break into my house in the middle of the night? What would you want with a weapon? Why would anyone buy fishing twine and a carving knife from the hardware store? What did I ever do to you?'

It occurred to Viktor that the accusations would be ludicrous if they weren't completely true. 'You even lied about your name!'

'I'm afraid you've lost me, Dr Larenz. Do you think

I've got some kind of grudge against you, is that the problem?'

'You tell me! According to Michael Burg, we've got "unfinished business"!'

'Are you feverish?'

*Of course I'm bloody feverish. Isn't that your intention?*

'I haven't said a word to Burg since he ferried me over.' Now Anna was losing her temper too. 'I don't know what you're talking about!'

She stood up and smoothed her trousers.

Someone was lying. Either Halberstaedt had made it up or Anna wasn't telling the truth.

'Fine,' she said furiously. 'If that's your opinion of me, we may as well end our sessions here.'

For the first time since their therapy started, Anna was beside herself with rage.

She grabbed her coat and bag and barged past him. Then she stopped in the hall and charged back in. Before Viktor could stop her, she took her revenge in the worst possible way.

Snatching the manila envelope from the desk, she hurled it into the fireplace. The paper went up in flames.

'No!'

Viktor wanted to sprint across the room, but couldn't muster the strength to take a single step.

'Why should you care about my story? You won't be seeing me again!'

'Stop!' he shouted after her, but Anna marched out

without looking back. The front door slammed behind her.

Anna Glass was gone for good – and with her any chance of finding out what had happened to Josy. The truth was smouldering in the fireplace, escaping through the chimney in a column of black smoke.

# 32

Groaning, Viktor dropped on to the couch.

What was going on? What was happening on the island?

He drew up his knees and hugged his shins.

Oh God.

He was sweating furiously and his old friend Mr Shivers had returned.

*What's wrong with me? I'll never find out the truth about Josy.*

You were being poisoned, said a voice inside him.

It was only paracetamol, his conscience replied.

It took a few moments for him to stop shaking and stand up.

The tea was cold by the time he summoned the strength to load the crockery on to a tray. He shuffled to the kitchen, staring at the cups in bewilderment. Distracted by the shocking evidence, he forgot to look where he was going, stumbled and let go of the tray. Everything crashed to the floor. Tea spilt everywhere, robbing him of the proof, but he knew for certain what he had seen.

*Both cups were full to the brim.*

He was willing to bet that Anna hadn't taken a single sip of tea.

Before he could fetch a dishcloth from the kitchen, a humming and rattling alerted him to the arrival of a fax on his old-fashioned machine.

Leaving the tray and broken china on the floor, he retraced his steps to the desk. Before he got there, he could tell there was a problem. The machine had disgorged a single piece of paper, which he picked up slowly and held under the lamp. He could turn it this way and that and study it for as long as he liked, but it wasn't going to get him any further. Not even a microscope would have helped. The fax was blank. There was no sign of a picture drawn by Josy, only a thick black line.

# 33

By the time Halberstaedt arrived with the awful news, Viktor was so worked up that he could barely remember his own telephone number, let alone Kai Strathmann's. The PI had failed to call about the fax. After waiting in vain for twenty minutes, Viktor had decided to ring Kai himself. Unfortunately, he was still so feverish that his memory seemed to be melting. Names and numbers were slopping around in his head like alphabet soup and it felt as if someone had given them a thorough stir. He couldn't remember Kai's number, so he couldn't ring him to tell him that the fax hadn't worked.

But the blank fax was the least of his problems. The thought that he might have been poisoned was driving him insane. His back felt excruciatingly tender, as if the skin had been burnt to a crisp, and his migraine had worked its way from the base of his skull to his forehead. Naturally, with the exception of himself, no one on Parkum knew anything about medicine, and the gusts had reached such a speed that even a military chopper would only leave the mainland in the event of an emergency. And he wasn't even sure that it *was* an emergency. Maybe Anna had been telling the truth and the powder was only paracetamol. Or maybe he had been poisoned in small doses, day by day.

*Like Charlotte? Like Josy?*

Had Anna had sufficient opportunity to poison him by degrees? He decided to give it a few more hours. The weather was atrocious and he didn't want the paramedics to risk their lives on his behalf. It would be unforgivable to make them fly through a hurricane if it turned out that he was suffering from the flu. Luckily he had packed some activated charcoal and other absorbent agents, which he took with some high-powered antibiotics, just in case.

Looking back on events, it occurred to Viktor that it was probably a good thing that he had been in a state of near physical exhaustion when Halberstaedt arrived with the shocking news. His brain, numbed by pain and the cocktail of tablets, was too weary and muddled to process the grisly details delivered to him on the porch.

'I'm sorry, Doctor,' said the mayor. He was holding a black cloth cap in both hands and spinning it with his fingers.

Viktor almost toppled over as he tried to crouch beside the body of his dog.

'I found Sindbad by the dustbins at the back of the Anchor.'

Viktor felt as if he were listening to a script from the wrong side of a theatre curtain. He knelt down and stroked the lifeless body of the golden retriever. It was obvious that the dog had been tortured. His hind legs, jawbone and maybe his spine were broken. 'You know who's staying there, don't you?'

'Pardon?' Viktor wiped the tears from his eyes and looked up at the mayor. Sindbad had been garrotted with a length of fishing twine that was buried in the flesh around his throat.

'Her, of course. That woman I warned you about. She's staying at the Anchor. You can bet your life she killed him.'

Viktor's instinct was to agree. He thought about asking Halberstaedt to wait while he fetched the gun so they could shoot her. Then he pulled himself together.

'Listen, Patrick, I don't want to talk about it. And I can't discuss the conduct of my patients.'

*Something fishy. Fishing twine.*

'You think she'll be back, do you? From what I saw, she was pretty het up when she left here. She was crying hysterically.'

'It's none of your business,' said Viktor in a strained, angry voice.

Halberstaedt raised his hands in surrender. 'Calm down, Doctor, I was only trying to help. You look pretty poorly.'

'It's hardly surprising, is it?'

'Even accounting for the fact that your dog has been murdered, you don't look yourself. Is there anything I can do?'

'No.' Viktor stared at the ravaged body of his dog. He

suddenly noticed the stab marks in its belly. The knife had penetrated the abdomen.

*A long blade, like a carving knife.*

'Actually, there is something you could do.' He got to his feet. 'You could bury Sindbad for me. I'm not up to it.' He didn't have the mental toughness, let alone the physical strength.

'No problem.' Halberstaedt tipped his cap at him. 'I'd best fetch a shovel.' He turned towards the toolshed and stopped. 'There's something else I wanted to show you. I'm hoping you'll take my warnings more seriously after this.'

'After what?'

Halberstaedt handed Viktor a green sheet of paper smeared with blood. 'It was in Sindbad's mouth when I found him.'

Viktor smoothed it out.

'It looks like a . . .'

'Exactly. It's a bank statement. And unless I'm much mistaken, it belongs to you.'

Viktor wiped away the blood in the top right-hand corner and was able to make out the name of his bank. It was a printout from his savings account where he and Isabell kept the bulk of their money.

'Read it carefully,' advised Halberstaedt.

The date and transaction number were printed on the left.

'That's today!'

'Apparently so.'

THERAPY

'But it can't possibly . . .' He knew there weren't any cash machines on Parkum. But it wasn't the date that concerned him most.

Two days ago the account balance had stood at 450,322 euros.

Yesterday someone had withdrawn the lot.

# 34

*Room 1245, Berlin-Wedding Psychosomatic Clinic*

'And it hadn't occurred to you until then that Isabell might be involved?'

Smoking was strictly forbidden in the clinic, but Dr Roth had fetched a cigarette for Viktor and was holding it next to his mouth.

'No, and even then I dismissed the idea straight away. It was simply too distressing.'

'And Isabell was the only one who could access the money?'

'Yes, the account was in both our names. If someone had withdrawn our savings, she must have authorized the transaction. Either that, or the bank had made a mistake.'

Dr Roth's bleep went off again, but this time he silenced it.

'Aren't you going to answer it?'

'It wasn't urgent.'

'I see. Only the wife,' chuckled Viktor.

Dr Roth wasn't amused. 'Let's focus on your spouse, Dr Larenz. Did you think about asking Kai to keep an eye on her?'

'Remember the hoo-ha about the forged Hitler diaries?' asked Viktor. 'Remember how the newspapers fell for the scam?'

'Yes.'

'Years ago I met a journalist who worked for *Stern*. He was directly involved with the story.'

'I'm not sure how this answers my question.'

'He and I were waiting in the green room at a TV studio where I was booked to appear on a talk show. He wasn't especially forthcoming about the diaries, but we met up later in the studio canteen and after a couple of beers he was ready to talk about it. I'll never forget what he said.'

'What?'

'He said: "We staked our reputations on those diaries. We'd risked too much for them not to be real. It was a case of seeing what we wanted to see: we were convinced they were genuine because the alternative was too awful to contemplate. We weren't looking for signs that we'd been conned; we were looking for proof that we were right."'

'How does that apply to you and Isabell?'

'I felt the same about my wife as he felt about the diaries: I wanted to trust her, so I did.'

'You didn't look into it any further?'

'Not right away. I had better things to do.' He took a drag on the cigarette that Dr Roth was holding for him.

'I had to get back to the mainland alive.'

# 35

'Help me, Viktor!'

Three words. And the first thought that crossed his mind was that Anna had dropped the 'doctor' from his name.

The horizon had closed in and was ominously close to the shore. Dark grey clouds hung heavy over the island, so low he could almost touch them, and the sky seemed intent on smothering the house. The full force of the storm was about to hit Parkum. By the time Viktor got out of bed to find out who was hammering on his door, the shipping forecast was reporting wind speeds of ten to twelve on the Beaufort scale. But Viktor was oblivious to the freakish weather raging around him. Before falling asleep, he had taken a couple of powerful sleeping pills in the hope of dozing for a few hours, free from pain or stress. When he opened the door, the parts of his nervous system that weren't under the numbing influence of the barbiturates were immediately focused on a new conundrum: Anna had turned up unexpectedly and Viktor had never seen such rapid deterioration in a patient's state of health. The woman who ninety minutes earlier had stormed out of his house in a fury was standing before him, hair matted, face wan and tired, and pupils dilated with fear. Her clothes, filthy and sodden, clung to her body, accentuating her pitiful state.

'Help me, Viktor.'

Those were her last three words that day. Before Viktor had time to react, she slumped to the ground, clutching helplessly at his blue woollen sweater. At first he thought she was having an epileptic fit. After all, there was a known link between epilepsy and psychosis. But, as he noted dispassionately, she wasn't trembling or flailing around. Nor was she displaying other typical symptoms such as foaming at the mouth or sudden incontinence. And she wasn't actually unconscious, just extremely dazed and unresponsive, as if she were spaced out on drugs.

Viktor made a snap decision to carry her into the house. Scooping her up from the wooden porch, he was surprised by how much she weighed. She seemed ridiculously heavy for someone of her build.

*I've really let myself go*, he thought, panting as he carried her to the spare room upstairs.

As he ascended the staircase, the pounding in his head grew deafeningly loud. It felt as if his body were soaking up the barbiturates, absorbing the manufactured tiredness like a sponge. He seemed to be getting more ponderous by the second.

The spare room was across the corridor from Viktor's bedroom. Fortunately he had arranged for all the beds to be made up prior to his arrival, so the room was ready for use.

He laid Anna between the white linen sheets and helped her out of her grimy cashmere coat. Then he loosened her silk scarf and took her pulse.

*No problems there.*

Following a sudden impulse, he opened her eyelids and shone a pen torch at her pupils. Anna clearly wasn't well. Both pupils responded sluggishly. That in itself wasn't a concern and could easily be a side effect of her medication, but it proved that she wasn't faking her condition. Anna was either sick or suffering from exhaustion. Like him.

What was wrong with them?

He decided not to think about it for the moment and to get on with removing her sodden clothes. He was a doctor, a doctor acting in the interest of his patient, but he still felt uncomfortable when it came to taking off her trousers, unbuttoning her blouse and slipping off her silk underwear. Her naked body was flawless. He wrapped her hastily in a fluffy white bathrobe from the bathroom and covered her with a light eiderdown quilt. She was so exhausted that she fell asleep before he finished tucking her in.

Viktor stayed for a while, listening carefully as his patient took deep, regular breaths. He was relieved to establish that she had suffered no more than a temporary breakdown and hadn't done herself serious harm.

All the same, the situation made him nervous.

He was ill and exhausted and now there was a

schizophrenic patient in his spare room who quite possibly wanted to kill him. As soon as she woke up, he intended to confront her about what had happened to Josy, Sindbad and his money.

Were it not for the sleeping pills and antibiotics sapping his strength, he would have erred on the side of caution and carried her back to the village without delay.

Viktor considered for a moment, then came to a decision. He went to the telephone to call for help.

Just as he picked up the receiver, a bolt of lightning flashed across the sky, illuminating the length of the beach. Viktor put down the phone and started counting. He only got as far as four when a deafening rumble shook the house. He hurried from room to room, unplugging electrical appliances in case of a power surge. After unplugging the television in the spare room, he waited for a moment, watching as Anna tossed, turned and sighed in her sleep. She seemed to be making a good recovery. In a couple of hours she would be back on her feet.

*She'll probably wake up while I'm asleep.*

He knew that he had to take action. The last thing he wanted was for Anna to hold him to ransom in his own house. He went downstairs to the telephone, pausing halfway to sit down for a moment and regain his balance.

When he got to the sitting room and picked up the phone, he was so exhausted that it took him a couple of seconds to realize that the line was dead. He put the handset back on the cradle and tried again, but the old-fashioned telephone refused to make a noise.

'Godawful weather, godawful island.'

The storm must have brought down the lines.

Viktor sat down on the couch and tried desperately to come up with an idea. He had a potentially violent patient in the house. He didn't have the strength to walk to the village. And the telephone didn't work. He could feel the numbing power of the barbiturates spreading through his system.

What was he to do?

In the very moment that he thought of a solution, he fell asleep.

# 36

This time it was different. The nightmare didn't follow its usual pattern; something had changed. For one thing, Josy wasn't in the Volvo as they raced down the pier towards the raging sea. At first he couldn't make out who was sitting on the back seat of the car. In his dream, he was intent on identifying the young woman who was drumming her fingers against the door. At last he recognized her:

Anna!

No one heard him shout because a hand was covering his mouth, stopping him from making a sound.

*What the hell is going on?*

Petrified, Viktor realized that the horrifying nightmare had given way to something indescribably worse. He was lying on the couch and the dream was real. He had woken up to find himself being smothered.

*I can't breathe*, he thought. He struck out, trying to shake off his attacker, but the sleeping pills, combined with the effects of his illness, conspired against him, robbing him of the strength to fight back. It felt as if an invisible force were pulling him downwards, pinning his arms to his side.

*This is it. She's going to kill me.*
*Halberstaedt was right.*

Grunting with exertion, he hurled himself to the side and kicked out wildly with one foot. He could feel himself being pushed further and further into the couch, then his foot connected with something soft and he heard an unnatural cracking and a muffled scream. Suddenly the hand lifted from his mouth and his lungs filled with air. The pressure on his chest was gone.

'Anna?' he shouted at the top of his voice, clutching at the air as if he were drowning. He slid off the couch and crawled across the floor.

'Anna!'

No answer.

*Maybe I'm still dreaming. Maybe none of this is real.*

Until now his thoughts had been clogged by flu and barbiturates, but at last he was starting to panic.

*Help! Light! I need light!*

'ANNA!'

On hearing his own voice, he felt like a diver gradually returning to the surface.

*Where's the bloody light?*

Straightening up unsteadily, he reached out and ran his fingers frantically over the wall. At last he found the light switch and the sitting room was flooded in bright yellow light from the four spotlights on the ceiling. He waited for his eyes to adjust and scanned the room.

*There's no one here. I'm on my own.*

He walked slowly to the window. It was closed. He

had almost reached his desk when the door slammed behind him. He whirled round. He could hear someone running barefoot up the stairs.

'Help me, Viktor!'

Three words uttered a few hours earlier by his unexpected guest. Now he repeated the sentence himself. He was in the grip of the same blind panic that had assailed him several times before. He stood rigid with shock, then stumbled to the door.

*What's happening to me? Was that her? Or am I dreaming?*

He stopped by the bureau in the hallway and rummaged around for the pistol. *Gone!*

Upstairs, heavy footsteps pounded across the landing.

He kept searching frantically and found the half-opened package at the back of the drawer, buried under a pile of handkerchiefs. Hands trembling, he ripped off the paper, grabbed two bullets and loaded the pistol. Spurred on by a rush of adrenalin, he sprinted upstairs.

Just as he reached the landing, the door to the spare room slammed shut. He ran to the end of the corridor.

'Anna, what are you . . .'

Viktor threw open the door and pointed the gun at the bed. He went to pull the trigger and caught his breath. The sight that greeted him was so shocking, so unexpected that it was more than he could handle in his present state.

He lowered the weapon.

*Impossible*, he thought, backing out of the room and

closing the door behind him. He was panting and gasping. *Impossible, completely impossible.*

It didn't add up, and worse still, he couldn't explain it. The spare room, the room where he had seen Anna sleeping peacefully, the room whose door she had slammed only moments earlier, was empty. And Anna was nowhere to be seen.

Half an hour later, when Viktor embarked on his second tour of the house to check the doors and windows, his fatigue had lifted. His uncontrolled shivering and rising temperature had cancelled out the effect of the sleeping pills. Besides, Anna had done her utmost to keep him awake. She had attacked him in his own living room and taken flight in the middle of a storm without stopping to get dressed. All her clothes and even his bathrobe were lying on the carpet in the spare room. She hadn't taken anything with her.

Viktor made himself a pot of strong coffee. Four questions were playing tag in his head:

*What does Anna want?*
*Did she really attack me?*
*Why did she run away?*
*Who is she?*

At half past four in the morning, he revived himself with a double dose of paracetamol and an ibuprofen. The day had only just begun.

# 37

## *Day of Reckoning, Parkum*

In certain situations, even the most rationally minded people behave in absurd and illogical ways. Nine times out of ten, a person in possession of a remote control will press the buttons harder if the battery runs low. But a nickel cadmium cell isn't like a lemon, and squeezing it firmly won't produce more juice.

In Viktor's opinion, the same could be said of the human brain. Exhaustion, illness and other factors were liable to drain a person's battery, thereby slowing his thoughts. In such circumstances, concentrating harder was futile: no amount of effort could force a synapse to generate a thought.

This was the attitude adopted by Viktor with regard to the previous night. None of what happened seemed to make sense. He could wrack his brains and consider the matter for as long as he liked, but poring over the details wasn't going to give him any answers and it certainly wasn't going to help his peace of mind.

*Charlotte, Sindbad, Josy. Murder.*

Everything hinged on a single question: *Who was*

*Anna Glass*? He needed to get to the truth before it was too late. At first he toyed with the idea of calling the police, but what evidence did he have? His dog was dead, he felt ill, someone had tried to kill him and his savings had disappeared. But he couldn't prove that Anna was involved.

On Monday morning, he would call the bank manager and put a block on his account. But it was only Sunday and he had neither the time nor the inclination to sit around and wait. He had to deal with the problem, and he had to deal with it alone. In spite of his near suffocation, he felt marginally better. But that was perturbing as well. What if his improved health were due to the fact that he had stopped drinking tea?

He was in the bathroom when he was startled by a strange noise. It came from downstairs. Someone was at the front door. This time it didn't sound like Halberstaedt's waders or Anna's high heels. Seized by a sudden, irrational fear, he closed his fingers around the pistol in his pocket, crept to the door and peered through the spyhole. Who would be out and about so early on a Sunday morning?

No one.

Viktor stood on tiptoe, then crouched down and peered under the door. Try as he might, he couldn't see anyone at all. He reached for the heavy brass handle, intending to open the door a centimetre or so. At that moment, he heard a rustling by his right foot. He glanced down and picked up an envelope that someone had slid through to him from outside.

It was a telegram. Years ago, at a time when no one had heard of email or faxes, Viktor wouldn't have been surprised to receive a telegram. But what was the point of a telegram when everyone could be contacted twenty-four hours a day by mobile phone? Surely telegrams were obsolete? True, he couldn't get a signal on Parkum, but he usually had a functioning landline and email as well. Why would anyone send him a telegram?

Viktor shoved the pistol into the pocket of his dressing gown and opened the door. Whoever had delivered the telegram was no longer in sight. The only living creature was a stray cat, its black fur wet and bedraggled, slinking towards the village. For a person to have disappeared like that would take an impressive burst of speed. The only cover was afforded by a forest of pine trees and spruces whose dripping branches seemed to block out the daylight.

Trembling, Viktor closed the door. He wasn't sure whether he was cold, frightened or ill. He discarded his sweat-drenched bathrobe and left it on the floor. After wrapping himself in a thick woollen cardigan from the coatrack in the hall, he opened the telegram, ripping the white envelope to get to the message. It consisted of a single sentence. He had to read it three times before it made sense and even then it made him gasp with shock.

SHAME ON YOU.

The message was printed in block capitals in a 12-point font on standard post office paper. The sender's details were listed at the bottom. He sat down slowly. The words seemed to blur before his eyes. *Isabell.*

Why on earth would Isabell send him a message like that? He turned the sheet over in his hands and examined it closely. It didn't make sense. *Shame on me for what?* What had he done? Had Isabell, who was still in Manhattan, found out something terrible about him? Had he done something so unspeakably dreadful that she couldn't bear to tell him on the phone? Why was she turning against him when he desperately needed her support?

Viktor decided to call her in New York. He went to the telephone and held the handset to his ear: still no dialling tone. The line, his only means of contacting his wife, was out of order.

*What are they playing at? They've had plenty of time to fix it by now.* He could only assume that the telephone masts had been damaged in the storm. Either that, or the high seas were affecting the underwater cables. Then, to his relief, he discovered a far simpler explanation. His instinct was to fix the problem and carry on, but then he was struck by a terrifying thought. The phone hadn't rung since Kai called two days ago. And the reason was obvious. Someone had disconnected it at the wall.

# 38

Isabell wasn't answering her phone, so Viktor decided to act. He couldn't sit at home all day waiting for her, Kai or Anna to call. It was time to take control.

It took him a few minutes to clear out the top drawer of the bureau in the hall. He was looking for a battered red notebook in which his father had compiled a directory of useful phone numbers. He read through the 'A's, then turned to 'G' for 'guesthouse'. He let it ring twenty-three times before he gave up.

He smiled wryly. *What do the Marriott Marquis in Times Square and the Anchor on Parkum have in common?*

He tried again, hoping that he had dialled the wrong number on his previous attempt. After a while the ringtone cut off of its own accord. No answer.

He stared out of the window. It was raining so heavily that he could barely see the long line of dark waves rolling in from the open water towards the beach.

Thumbing nervously through the notebook, he read through the entries under 'H'.

This time he was in luck. Halberstaedt, unlike Trudi and Isabell, was prepared to take his call.

'Good morning, Patrick. I'm terribly sorry for disturbing you at home. I've been thinking about the advice you gave me, and if the offer still stands, I'd appreciate your help.'

'The advice I gave you,' echoed Halberstaedt, puzzled. 'I'm afraid I don't follow.'

'Under normal circumstances, I wouldn't think twice about walking there myself, but what with the rain and everything, I was hoping you might pop next door and . . .'

'And what?'

'Tell Anna that I need to speak to her. It's urgent.'

'Speak to who?'

'Anna,' said Viktor. 'Anna Glass.'

'Never heard of her.'

Viktor detected a low whistling in his right ear. It seemed to be getting louder.

'Come on, Patrick, you said you knew she was dangerous as soon as she got off the boat. You accused her of killing my dog.'

'You must be mistaken, Dr Larenz.'

'Mistaken? I've lost count of the number of times you warned me about her. You insisted on keeping an eye on her. Remember what she did to Sindbad?'

'But I haven't seen you all week – or Sindbad, for that matter. Are you sure you're all right?'

The noise was loud enough to be tinnitus. It had spread to his left ear.

'Listen, Patrick, I don't know what the hell you're—'

Viktor stopped abruptly and listened to the voice in the background.

'Is that her?'

'Who?'

'Anna. Is she there?'

'Dr Larenz, I don't know what you're talking about. I'm on my own here, as usual.'

Viktor gripped the handset with the desperation of a drowning man clinging to a lifebuoy.

'But that's ... I mean, it's not...' He didn't know what to say. Then he had a sudden thought. 'Hang on a moment.'

He ran back to the hall and picked up his dressing gown. To his relief, he found what he was looking for: the loaded gun. It was in the pocket where he had left it, proof that he wasn't going mad.

He ran back to the phone.

'Listen, Patrick, I've had enough of this nonsense. I'm standing here with your pistol.'

'Oh.'

'Is that all you've got to say? Aren't you going to tell me what's going on?' demanded Viktor, raising his voice to a shout.

'Well I ... The thing is, I ...' stuttered Halberstaedt.

Viktor heard the change in his voice and knew at once that someone was with him, telling him what to say.

'All right, Patrick, I don't know what you're playing at, but I'm running out of time. I need to speak to Anna immediately. Tell her to meet me in her room at the

Anchor in an hour. Come to think of it, you should probably join us. We may as well get things out in the open.'

He heard a sigh. Then the voice changed again. The mayor's nervous, almost grovelling tone was gone. 'Don't be ridiculous, Dr Larenz,' he snapped with unbearable arrogance. 'Like I said, I don't know any Annas. And even if I did, you'd be wasting your time at the Anchor.'

'What do you mean?'

'It's been closed for weeks. There's no one there, not even Trudi.'

The line went dead.

# 39

Searching for truth is like putting together a jigsaw without knowing how many pieces are in the box.

Viktor had begun by assembling a framework of questions. Now he was working from the outside in, which meant coming up with answers to impossible questions like:

*Why was he feeling ill?*

*Who killed Sindbad?*

*What was the connection between Halberstaedt and Anna?*

And:

*Who was Anna Glass?*

A single phone call could have answered the latter, but he didn't have time to make it. The phone rang just as he was reaching for the handset.

'Who is she?'

*At long last!* He was so overcome with relief that he didn't know what to say.

'Who is she, Viktor?'

'Isabell!' he exclaimed, finally finding his voice. He didn't know what to make of her aggressive tone. 'I'm so pleased you phoned. Did you get my messages? They wouldn't put me through.'

'Uh-huh, I bet you were desperate to speak to me!'

'Yes, I spoke to the staff at reception. What's the matter? I couldn't make sense of your telegram. You sound angry with me.'

'Ha!' There was a furious silence, punctuated only by the crackling of the transatlantic line.

'Darling,' said Viktor nervously, 'why don't you tell me what's wrong?'

'Don't call me darling! Not after what happened yesterday!'

Viktor was beginning to lose his temper. He held the receiver to his other ear. 'Perhaps you could stop yelling and tell me what I've done.'

'Fine, if you're going to play games, I'll have to spell it out. Let's start with a simple question: what's the name of your little tart?'

Viktor laughed out loud. He could literally feel a ten-ton weight being lifted from his shoulders. So that was why Isabell was angry: she thought he was having an affair.

'Don't laugh like a little kid. And don't treat me like an idiot.'

'But that's not ... Isabell, please! You know I'd never cheat on you. Whatever gave you that idea?'

'I specifically asked you not to treat me like an idiot. Tell me who she is!'

'I don't know what you're talking about,' said Viktor, angry again.

'I'm talking about *her*, the woman who picked up the phone when I called the house yesterday.'

Viktor blinked in confusion, still trying to process what she was saying. 'Yesterday?'

'Yes, yesterday! Half past two in the afternoon if you must know.'

*Anna. She was here in the afternoon. But she couldn't have . . .*

Viktor's mind was racing. For a moment he experienced a sensation of giddiness as if he were disembarking from a long-haul flight.

'How long have you been seeing her? All those lines you fed me about needing space, needing time to reflect. You're despicable; pretending to work on an interview when really you were using our daughter's memory to cover up your sordid affair!'

*I was watching Anna the whole time. The whole time except . . .*

*The phone rang in the kitchen. She was meddling with my tea.*

The memory of Anna in the sitting room returned to him like a boomerang, taking him by surprise. He sat down abruptly.

*But I only left her for a second . . .*

'Anna.'

'I see, Anna. And her surname?'

'What?'

He hadn't realized that he had spoken out loud.

'Listen, Isabell, you've got it all wrong. She's not my mistress.'

*Oh God, I sound like a cheating husband who's sleeping with his secretary. Don't worry, it's not what it looks like.*

'Anna is a patient.'

'You're sleeping with a patient?' Isabell was becoming hysterical.

'Good heavens, no! Our relationship is strictly professional.'

'Strictly professional?' More loud, mocking laughter. 'Of course it is! In that case, perhaps you'd like to explain what she's doing in our house! You're not seeing patients anymore, remember? And what would a patient be doing on Parkum? For Christ's sake, Viktor, this is so humiliating. I'm going to hang up.'

'Please, Isabell, I can see why you're angry, but give me a chance to explain. I'm begging you.'

Silence. The ear-splitting siren of a New York ambulance echoed across the Atlantic Ocean.

'If I knew what was going on here, I'd tell you. But you've got to believe me: I'm not sleeping with the woman who spoke to you on the phone. All I can tell you for certain is that I'd never cheat on you, never. You'll have to trust me because I can't explain the rest. Five days ago there was a knock on the door and a woman calling herself Anna Glass asked for a consultation. She said she was a children's writer suffering from schizophrenic delusions. I don't know how she tracked me down and I don't know where she is now, but her condition sounded so unusual, so intriguing that I agreed to give her therapy. She was supposed to leave Parkum four days ago but she's trapped on the island because of the storm.'

'Interesting story. You've got quite an imagination,' snapped Isabell.

'It's not a story, it's the truth! She had no right to answer the phone. I popped into the kitchen and I guess she must have picked it up without me knowing.'

'It didn't ring.'

'Pardon?'

'She got to the phone before it rang. She must have been waiting for someone to call.'

Viktor felt as if someone was pulling a rug from under his feet. There was something strange about Anna Glass; something he couldn't begin to fathom.

'Isabell, I don't get it either. The strangest things have been happening since she arrived. I fell ill, someone attacked me, and I think Anna knows what happened to Josy.'

'What?'

'She knows something about Josy. I've been trying to contact you for days. I wanted to tell you that we might have a lead. Kai's on the case again. And someone withdrew all our savings. I thought you might be able to help me, but I couldn't get hold of you, and then this morning I got your telegram.'

'*I've* been trying to contact *you*. That's why I sent a telegram.'

*The phone was disconnected.*

'I know. Someone disconnected the phone.'

'Please, Viktor, don't insult my intelligence. A woman appears out of nowhere, she tells you a story about our daughter, she waits by our phone, says something she shouldn't, and disconnects the call. Is that honestly the best you can do? A story about a drunken one-night stand would have been more convincing!'

Viktor didn't hear the last sentence. An alarm bell had sounded halfway through Isabell's tirade. *Said something she shouldn't?*

'What did she say to you?'

'At least she had the decency not to lie. She said you were in the shower.'

'But I wasn't! I was in the kitchen, talking to Kai. Then I told her to leave,' protested Viktor. He was on the verge of hysteria and he shouted the next sentence at the top of his voice. 'I barely know the woman: she's a patient!'

'She seems to know you pretty well.'

'What's that supposed to mean?'

'She called you by your pet name. The name your mother gave you, the name you supposedly hate so much that you've never told anyone apart from me!'

'Diddy?'

'That's right! And you know what, Diddy? You can go to hell!'

With that, she slammed down the phone. A single monotonous tone sounded from the handset.

# 40

Never before had Viktor felt so trapped, so hunted as he was feeling now. Anna had invaded every aspect of his life. She wasn't the first to cross the line and harass him at home, but usually there was a clear, although by no means rational, explanation as to why a patient should take an interest in his personal affairs. In Anna's case, the threat was veiled and inscrutable. He couldn't understand what she wanted from him or why she was using a false name – the name of a student who had been poisoned. Why had she lied to him and to Isabell? And, more importantly, what did she know about Josy?

Viktor had a feeling that he was missing something. The events of the past five days were undoubtedly linked. Everything that had happened was part of a strategy whose goal would become apparent if he could figure out where each episode belonged in the chain. He hadn't succeeded so far.

Mercifully, he seemed to be recovering from his illness, probably because it was twenty-four hours since his last cup of tea.

He took a long shower and pulled on some clothes.

*I suppose I should do some washing*, he thought as he

picked up yesterday's jeans. He turned out the pockets and threw away the mountain of used tissues. A slip of paper fluttered to the floor. Even as he stooped down, he knew exactly what it was: the note that had dropped out of Anna's wallet several days earlier. In his panic, he had scooped it up, stuffed it into his pocket and forgotten about it. The tiny rectangle of folded paper reminded him of a love note passed between teenagers at school. He didn't know what he expected it to say, but it was profoundly disappointing. Written across the note was a series of digits. For all he knew, it could be anything: the code for a safety deposit box, an account number, an Internet password, or more probably, a phone number.

*A phone number!*

He hurried downstairs as fast as he could and picked up the phone in the kitchen. Slowly, he dialled the number and prepared himself to hang up as soon as someone answered. He only wanted to find out their name.

# 41

'Dr Larenz, what a relief!'

Viktor was so surprised to be greeted by name that he didn't hang up. He hadn't reckoned with the person on the other end knowing who he was. Apart from anything else, his old-fashioned analogue phone wasn't compatible with caller ID. Whose number had he called? How had the person on the other end of the line known that it was him? And why had they been waiting for him to call?

'What is it?' he asked, trying to give away as little as possible. He didn't want to confirm his identity just yet.

'I didn't want to bother you, not after what you've been through, but I'm afraid it's rather urgent.'

The voice sounded oddly familiar.

'I thought I should tell you before it got out of hand.'

*Professor van Druisen!* Viktor finally recognized his friend and mentor's voice. But what was his number doing in Anna's wallet?

'Van Druisen! Is something the matter?'

'Didn't you get my email?'

Email? Viktor hadn't logged on for days. His inbox would be overflowing by now. There were bound to be several messages from *Bunte*: he had missed the deadline for the interview.

'No, I haven't had time to check my mail. Is there a problem?'

'I had a break-in about a week ago.'

'A break-in? I'm sorry to hear it, Professor, but I don't see what it's got to do with me.'

'It wasn't an ordinary burglary. Very little was taken, which makes it more disturbing. Only one cabinet was broken into. I'm missing a single file.'

'Patient notes?'

'Yes, but the question is, whose? It was the cabinet where I archived the files that I inherited from your practice. It seems to me that someone might be targeting one of your former patients.'

'But if you don't know whose file is missing, how can you be sure that it's missing at all?'

'A binder was found in the corridor. Whoever took it was cunning enough to rip off the labels. All the documents are missing and there's no way of telling whose notes were inside.'

Viktor closed his eyes as if to shut down his other senses and focus his attention on what he had heard. Why would anyone want to steal a set of ancient case notes? Who would break into a psychiatrist's office to get their hands on an archived file? It seemed to Viktor that there was only one person who fitted the bill. He opened his eyes.

'Listen carefully, Professor. I'm going to ask you

something important. Does the name Anna Glass mean anything to you?'

'Oh God, so you know.'

'Know what?'

'About Anna . . . I mean, I thought you . . .'

Viktor had never heard the distinguished professor fumbling over his words.

'You thought *what*?'

'I thought . . . Hang on, you're the one who mentioned her first.'

'Anna. Anna Glass. Did you send her to see me? Did you give her my address?'

'She didn't come to you, did she? Oh Lord.'

'She turned up on Parkum. Maybe you could tell me what's going on.'

'I said this would happen, I always knew it was a mistake. I should never have agreed to it.' There was a desperate edge to van Druisen's voice. It almost sounded as if he were whimpering.

'With respect, Professor, I'd like to know what's going on.'

'My dear Larenz, you're in danger.'

Viktor gripped the receiver like a tennis player on the baseline, bracing himself to return the serve.

'What kind of danger?'

'Anna Glass was a patient of mine. I would never have taken her on if she hadn't been recommended by a friend.'

'She's schizophrenic, isn't she?'

'Is that what she told you?'

'Yes.'

'It's a ploy of hers.'

'So there's nothing wrong with her?'

'On the contrary, she's extremely disturbed. She claims to be schizophrenic, but she's not. That's her pathology, so to speak.'

'What do you mean?'

'Did she tell you about the time she killed a dog?'

'Terry. She said it was her first schizophrenic episode.'

'Not exactly. Ms Glass wasn't hallucinating: she killed her own dog. She says she's schizophrenic because it's easier than confronting the truth.'

'So the things she told me were . . .'

'A hundred per cent true. Her way of living with the past is to hide behind an imaginary illness. She won't face up to the terrible things she's done. Do you see what we're dealing with?'

'Yes.'

*The story about Charlotte, her nocturnal appearance in his house, the trip to Hamburg, the poisoning – it was all true . . .*

'Did you give her my address?'

'Surely you know me better than that? Ms Glass wasn't welcome in my practice and I wouldn't dream of referring her to a friend. Besides, you made it perfectly clear that you weren't seeing any patients! No, the fact is that Anna Glass missed her last appointment. Strangely enough, it was the day of the break-in – and if you ask me, she was involved.'

'What makes you say that?'

'She mentioned your name on numerous occasions. She said you had "unfinished business"; those were her words. During our last few sessions she even talked about poisoning you.'

Viktor swallowed and realized that his throat felt normal for the first time in days.

'Poisoning me? But why? I don't even know who she is.'

'She seems to know you.'

Viktor was reminded of what Isabell had said a few moments earlier. Everyone seemed to think he was connected to Anna Glass.

'She talked about you all the time. I blame myself for not taking her seriously. I think she might be dangerous; in fact, I'm certain of it. She told me the most dreadful things. She's hurt people before, you know. I can't bear to think about what happened to that innocent little girl.'

'Charlotte?'

'I think that's what she called her. I feel terrible, Dr Larenz, really terrible. I should have followed my instincts and sent her somewhere else. She needs twenty-four-hour supervision.'

'Surely you could have found a suitable institution?'

'My dear Larenz, you know perfectly well that I . . .' The professor broke off, suddenly embarrassed.

'What?'

'I couldn't just get rid of her.'

'Why not?'

'Because of what I promised your wife. I gave her my word.'

'My wife?' Viktor felt himself swaying and steadied himself on the fridge.

'Yes, Isabell asked me to treat her. I couldn't let her down. Not when she and Anna are so close.'

# 42

Isabell. Anna. Josy. The pieces of the jigsaw were falling into place. At last he was beginning to see how Isabell had managed to keep her cool when Josy vanished. She had coped with the news much better than he had, returning to work without a second thought. Viktor, who had sold his practice and never recovered from the shock, used to admire her for her strength, but now he saw that she was simply callous.

His thoughts drifted to and fro. Looking back on her behaviour, he realized that Isabell had never grieved for her only child – not in the way that he had. He wondered whether she had found Sindbad by chance, as she had claimed, or whether she had picked him up from a rescue centre to replace their little girl. What sort of a person was Isabell? And why wouldn't she support him through this, the most stressful period of his life?

Isabell had sent Anna to Professor van Druisen.

And someone had withdrawn the savings from their account.

Viktor sat down at his desk and booted up his laptop. He needed to check his balance online. It didn't seem possible that Isabell had cleaned out their joint account.

Was she in league with Anna? Together they seemed determined to torment him.

After scanning his desktop vainly for the Internet Explorer icon, he dragged the mouse to the bottom of the screen. He stared at the computer in confusion.

The task bar was empty and the icons had gone.

He decided to try the start menu instead. The short-cuts had been deleted. Worse still, there was no sign of the programs. The hard drive had been wiped clean.

Someone had been through his laptop systematically and deleted his personal documents, case notes and folders, including the half-finished interview. Even the recycle bin, which usually contained copies of recently deleted data, was empty.

Viktor stood up so abruptly that the leather chair flew back, tipped over and came to rest beside the bookcase. He was past caring. The time for phone calls was over. Even his missing savings could wait.

He took out the pistol that Halberstaedt had given him, released the safety catch, and tucked it into the inside pocket of his Gore-tex jacket. It was just as well he had brought his waterproofs.

*Don't delay.*

He steeled himself to fight his way through the storm to the village in search of two things:

Anna Glass and the truth.

# 43

People feel the cold in different ways. Some are kept awake when their toes refuse to warm up even after vigorous jiggling under the bedclothes. Others are cursed with sensitive noses.

Viktor's weak spot was his ears. In winter they seemed to hurt from the moment he left the house. But the discomfort of frozen ears was nothing compared to the agony of letting them thaw. As soon as he returned to the warmth, the earache migrated across the back of his skull, starting at the base and spreading upwards in a wave of pain that no amount of aspirin or ibuprofen could conquer. As a child, he had learnt the hard way to take care of his ears, and now, as he trudged towards the village, he saw to it that the drawstrings were pulled as tight as possible on his hood. He didn't especially mind the rain; his priority was to keep out the cold.

And so it was that his hood blocked out the tinny melody barely audible amid the howling wind swirling around him, whipping up the sand and leaves. In fact, if he hadn't left the hopelessly flooded track to shelter under the eaves of Parkum's old customhouse, he might never have heard the ringing in his jacket pocket. He wasn't expecting any calls: there were no mobile-phone masts on the island, and he saw little point in checking his phone. And yet, as he realized as soon as he pushed back his hood, someone was calling him.

He glanced at the screen. The number looked familiar.

'Hello?'

He held the phone to his right ear and stuck a finger in the other because of the deafening wind. There didn't seem to be anyone on the line.

'Hello? Can you hear me?'

The wind dropped for a moment and Viktor thought he heard a sob.

'Anna? Is that you?'

'I'm sorry, Dr Larenz, I . . .'

At precisely that moment a heavy branch gave in to the storm and crashed on to the roof overhead. Viktor missed the end of her sentence.

'Anna, where are you?'

'I'm . . . Anchor . . .'

The snippets of information didn't add up to much, but he was determined to keep her on the line.

'Listen, Anna, I know you're not staying at the Anchor. Patrick Halberstaedt told me so. Why don't you text me your exact location? I'll be there in a few minutes and we can talk face to face. It's much better than on the—'

'She's back!'

Anna screamed the last sentence just as the hurricane granted the battered island a brief respite. A moment later the wind returned with devastating fury.

'Who's back?'

'Charlotte . . . She's on the . . .'

Viktor didn't need to hear anymore. He knew exactly what she was trying to tell him. Anna was having another schizophrenic episode. Charlotte had come alive.

Viktor was so absorbed in his thoughts that it took a couple of minutes for him to realize that the line had gone dead. He stared uncomprehendingly at the screen: no reception. And yet the beep-beep of his Nokia handset heralded the arrival of a text:

'Don't try looking for me. I'LL GET TO YOU!'

# 44

The real reason why most drivers hate sitting in traffic is because it makes them feel powerless to decide their fate. The natural reaction to seeing a queue of stationary lights is to look for a means of escape. For some people, the thought of getting stuck is so distressing that turning off and picking their way through unknown back roads seems better than waiting for the traffic to clear.

Viktor had reached a stage where he could either join the Friday afternoon rush hour or take the next exit and strike out alone. Like most people, he couldn't bear the thought of waiting passively, so he decided to act. Anna had warned him not to look for her, but he wasn't prepared to hang around while she called the shots. He needed to find her while he still had the chance.

And so, hood pulled up and leaning into the wind, he set off towards the village. He cheated the storm by keeping as low as possible and weaving around the puddles that pitted the sandy track.

He had long since passed the island's solitary restaurant and was only five hundred metres from the marina when he stopped abruptly and scanned his surroundings. He could have sworn there was someone up ahead.

He wiped away the raindrops and shielded his eyes with his hand.

*There.*

It was just as he had thought. Twenty or so metres away, a figure in a blue raincoat was battling through the storm and dragging something behind them on a leash.

At first he wasn't able to tell the person's gender – or whether they were walking towards him or away. Even at close range it was almost impossible to see anything because of the rain. A flash of lightning seared over the waves, lighting up the track. By the time the thunder followed, Viktor knew who was approaching and what was on the lead.

'Michael, is that you?' he shouted to the ferryman when he was only a couple of paces away. The wind was howling so furiously that neither could hear the other until they were close enough to touch.

Michael Burg was seventy-one years old and looked every day of it, although it was difficult to tell because of the pouring rain. The wind and salt had left deep furrows in his leathery skin, but in spite of his weathered face he had the robust look of someone who had spent a lifetime outdoors in the bracing sea air.

He held out his left hand. In his right he was holding the end of a leash to which a drenched and shivering schnauzer was attached.

'My wife reckoned he needed a walk,' he bellowed

into the wind, shaking his head as if to say that only a woman could come up with such a stupid idea. Viktor thought of Sindbad and winced.

'And you? What are you doing out in this weather?' asked Burg.

Lightning blazed across the sky and for a brief moment Viktor had a clear view of the ferryman who was looking at him with undisguised suspicion.

He decided to tell the truth, not because he felt an obligation to be honest, but because he couldn't think why else he would be risking his life by walking across the island in the middle of a furious storm.

'I'm looking for someone. Perhaps you can help me.'

'I'll do my best. Who is it?'

'Anna. Anna Glass. Small, blonde, mid-thirties. She got here three days ago. You ferried her over from Sylt.'

'Three days ago? I don't know where you got your information, but you must have heard wrong.'

From the ferryman's tone, Viktor could tell that he shared his bemusement. He wondered how many times he had felt the same mixture of disbelief and foreboding during the past few hours.

Burg's black schnauzer was already straining at the leash. It was shivering more wretchedly than before and seemed to share its owner's dim view of the weather, especially now they were standing still.

'What do you mean?' It seemed to Viktor that he was obliged to shout louder and louder to make himself heard.

'I haven't had the boat out in three weeks.' He shrugged. 'Business is quiet at this time of year – no one visits Parkum in winter. The last person I ferried over was you.' He seemed anxious to leave.

'Then how the hell did she get here?' demanded Viktor.

'On another boat, I guess, although normally I'd hear about it. What did you say she was called again?'

'Glass. Anna Glass.'

Burg shook his head. 'Never heard of her. Sorry, Dr Larenz, but we'll catch our death in this weather.'

As if to underscore his words, a deep rumbling sounded from the north of the island. Part of Viktor wondered why he hadn't seen the lightning, while the other grappled with the next piece of the jigsaw. How had Anna arrived on Parkum? And why had she lied?

Viktor's thoughts were interrupted by the old ferryman who had taken a couple of steps, then stopped.

'Err, Dr Larenz, I know it's none of my business, but what do you want with her?'

Burg didn't need to articulate the full question; Viktor could feel its oppressive presence in the stormy air. *Why would a married man be searching for a young woman in the driving rain?*

He shrugged and walked away. *I want to know what happened to my daughter.*

# 45

The Anchor was everything that visitors expected from a boarding house on a quiet North Sea island. With the exception of the lighthouse at Struder Point, the charming three-storeyed timber building was one of the tallest on Parkum and the front windows looked out over the marina. Trudi had run the business single-handed since her husband's death and her modest pension, together with the takings from the handful of summer tourists, allowed her to keep the place afloat. As far as the islanders were concerned, the Anchor was an institution, and their commitment to its survival was absolute. Most of them would have moved in with their belongings rather than lose the hub of village life. The best days were during sailing regattas when the Anchor would accommodate up to twenty guests. And when it was sunny enough, which wasn't that often, Trudi would move the dining tables into the garden and serve home-made lemonade and iced coffee to tourists and friends. As soon as autumn came, the older islanders would gather in the lobby and swap sailors' yarns around the wrought-iron stove while Trudi fed them cake – unless she decided to escape the Parkum winter and stay with relatives until the spring. And that, as Viktor had gathered from his strange conversation with Halberstaedt, was exactly what she had done. Walking slowly towards the building, he saw without surprise that the shutters were down and the chimney was out of action.

He looked around for signs of Anna. *I should have saved myself the trouble*, he thought grimly.

For a moment he was tempted to call her name in case she had broken into the Anchor and was playing another of her games.

Just then his mobile rang. This time it was the ringtone for family and friends.

'Hello?'

'Is this your idea of a joke?'

'Kai? Has something happened?' Viktor left the boarding house and headed down the track in an easterly direction. He was taken aback by the PI's tone.

'You've got a sick sense of humour.'

'I don't know what you mean.'

'The fax, Viktor, the fax.'

'Oh, I tried to call you. It was blank.'

'Then fax yourself another one. I'm not as stupid as you think.'

'I don't think you're stupid. Kai, what's going on?'

A sudden gust drove a flurry of raindrops into Viktor's face. He swivelled round and looked back at the Anchor. From this angle, the empty boarding house looked like a cardboard facade on a film set.

'I traced the fax. I mean, who the hell would send me a picture of a cat?'

*Josy's cat. Nepomuk.*

'Well?'

'It was you. The picture was sent from your number. You faxed it from your house.'

*That's impossible*, thought Viktor.

'Listen, Kai, I don't know what to—' He heard a series of beeps and realized that the line was dead. An automated voice told him to hang up and try again later.

'Damn.' Viktor checked his mobile and cursed his bad luck. Without a signal, he could forget about calling the mainland. He whirled round and stood with his back to the Anchor, surveying the land ahead. He finished up by staring at the sky, as if the solution were written in the ominous black clouds.

Who would help him now? Was there anyone left to trust? A plump raindrop hit him straight in the eye. Blinking frantically, he was reminded of sitting in the bath and screwing up his eyes to get rid of the shampoo. He ran a hand over his face and was surprised to find that he could see more clearly. Everything looked much sharper, as if the optician had chosen the right lens and brought the bottom row of letters into focus. Or maybe it was merely coincidence that a moment later he knew exactly what to do.

# 46

Just as Viktor had expected, the lights were still on in the mayor's cottage. He ran up the steps to the porch and held down the doorbell.

He could hear a dog, probably the ferryman's schnauzer, barking in the distance, and something – either a gate or a shutter – was banging in the wind. But he couldn't say for certain whether the bell had actually rung. He gave it another minute in case Halberstaedt was already on the way to the door.

When the second ring produced no reaction, he dispensed with politeness and banged the hefty knocker impatiently against the cedar door. Halberstaedt's wife had left him two years earlier for a rich guy from Munich, and now he lived alone.

Still no response.

*Bloody wind. I don't suppose he can hear me*, thought Viktor as he circled the house. It was situated in a prime location, right next to the Anchor and overlooking the marina, but it didn't have a jetty or beach access, and Halberstaedt had to cross the narrow coast road in order to get to the sea. Of course, it didn't much matter on a tiny island like Parkum, but Viktor was of the opinion that seaside houses should be located directly on the beach. Otherwise he would rather save himself the trouble and stay on the mainland near a lake.

The wind was battering the island from the sea, and it came as a relief to Viktor when he rounded the corner and found himself sheltered by the house.

Until then he had been pummelled constantly by the gusts, shielded only by a handful of pathetic-looking pine trees, their slender trunks bent double from the stormy North Sea weather. Now that he was tucked behind the house, the rain decided to let up a little and he could afford to catch his breath. He allowed himself to rest a short while, then resumed his hunt for the mayor.

The large window at the back belonged to the study, but Halberstaedt had obviously gone upstairs. The desk was strewn with innumerable pages of handwritten notes, and a laptop had been abandoned, still open, on a stool. There was no sign of life and in the hearth the fire was burning low. In fact, Viktor had almost given up hope when he noticed that the desk lamp was still alight. *He can't have gone out*, he thought to himself.

He couldn't imagine why Halberstaedt needed a study, much less a computer.

A quick glance at the rest of the house was enough to determine that the lights were out upstairs. Of course, that didn't mean anything: if Halberstaedt were up there, he was more than likely to be in bed, in which case the curtains would be pulled.

Viktor was running out of ideas. So far he had achieved precisely nothing apart from getting wet. But that was entirely predictable, given that he had no idea of Anna's location or what to do if he tracked her down.

*Don't try looking for me. I'LL GET TO YOU!*

Viktor decided to knock one last time. Then he noticed a shed at the bottom of the overgrown garden.

Under normal circumstances, the faint light leaking under the corrugated-iron door wouldn't have caught his attention, but the past hours had taken such a toll on his body that his mind was working overtime. He registered several things at once: the shed was lit up, the only window was boarded over on the inside, and smoke was rising from the narrow metal chimney atop the flat roof.

What would persuade Halberstaedt to go out to his shed in the pouring rain? And who in their right mind would block up a shed window while leaving the lights on and curtains open in their house?

Viktor had a vague feeling that something bad was about to happen, but he swallowed his doubts and hurried over the waterlogged lawn. He was going to find out what Halberstaedt was up to in the shed.

## 47

The door wasn't locked. He opened it slowly and was enveloped in thick, fusty air. The shed smelt of oil, old rags and mouldering wood, an odour that pervades every neglected basement or workshop. With the exception of a few beetles and woodlice that scuttled for cover when he appeared from the rain, the shed was deserted.

But Halberstaedt wasn't the only notable absence. To Viktor's surprise, there wasn't a single tool in the shed. No spades, rakes or trowels, no half-empty tins of paint on the chipboard shelves, no building materials abandoned on the floor.

In spite of its generous size, as large as a double garage, the shed didn't house so much as a wheelbarrow, let alone an old rowing boat or an ancient bike. But it wasn't merely the lack of everyday equipment that was making him shiver. Viktor felt cold all over. Throughout the long walk from his cottage into the wind he hadn't noticed the chill in the air, but as soon as he entered the hidden hut at the bottom of the mayor's garden he felt frozen to the bone. The cold started in the small of his back and crept up his spine, spreading across his scalp and through the rest of his body, giving him goosebumps.

*Death is always cold.*

Viktor gave himself a little shake, partly to make sure he wasn't dreaming, and partly to dispel the oppressive thoughts attacking his mind. He had just realized what was going on.

What he would have given to be at home, wherever that was. At home, sitting with his wife by the fire, or in a warm bath surrounded by candles. At home, shielded from the world by solid doors and shuttered windows. At home, or anywhere but here, as far away as possible from the hundreds of photos and newspaper articles taunting him from all sides.

Someone – Halberstaedt or Anna – had covered the walls with a monstrous collage of pictures, captions and articles collected over the course of many months. The subject matter wasn't conventionally abhorrent. There were no blood-spattered bodies, sexual perversions or graphic images from X-rated websites, but the clippings shared a common theme, a theme that filled him with dread. There were photos everywhere – tacked to the walls, pinned to the shelves, and pegged on washing lines suspended across the shed – and everywhere he looked he saw Josy.

It was like stumbling into a paper maze of memories and being trapped by his daughter's gaze. The shed was a shrine to a pathological obsession. Someone had spent their free time researching Josy's abduction. His daughter was the object of an irrational and monstrous cult.

The ancient light bulb dangling from the ceiling bathed the clippings in uncertain light. Viktor overcame his revulsion and examined the collage more closely.

At first he thought he was imagining things, then he realized the newspaper was stained with bloody finger-prints. Delicate fingerprints; too delicate for someone with Halberstaedt's bear-like hands.

But the captions were what persuaded Viktor that he was looking at the work of an unsound mind. Each headline had been cut to size, highlighted with a coloured marker and glued to a photo.

Wrapping his right hand in his scarf to protect it from the heat, he reached up and tilted the bulb towards the wall. The captions came into focus.

PSYCHIATRIST'S DAUGHTER GOES MISSING

SHRINK IN NIGHTMARE TRAUMA

TV DOCTOR ABANDONED BY WIFE

WHO POISONED LITTLE JOSY?

LARENZ VERDICT: PSYCHIATRIST BANNED!

*What kind of sick person would make up nonsense like that?* Some of the headlines were genuine, but for the most part they were fabrications – and increasingly preposter-ous ones at that.

*It must have been her.*

He couldn't imagine the time it must have taken to think up the headings, print them out in newspaper style and arrange them on the walls. And he was baffled by the photos. Some of them had been downloaded from the web, but others he had never seen before.

Anna must have been stalking his family long before Josy disappeared. Had she taken the photos without their knowledge? It was still too early to prove anything, but Viktor was certain that he was looking at Anna's work.

*I need to read the captions*, he decided, angling the bulb to the left. *If I study them carefully, I might find the key to what she wants.*

If he hadn't been so intent on inspecting the collage, events might have taken a different turn. Perhaps he would have heard the rustling in the garden instead of staring, deep in thought, at the cryptic messages on the wall. He might have left the shed and never noticed the sheet of paper that made him cry out in horror and stopped him from hearing the sound of cracking twigs. With a bit of luck, he might have turned round and spotted the danger. Who knows.

Instead he let go of the light bulb and tore down the offending piece of paper that was tacked to the wall by a rusty nail. He didn't stop to read its contents. The alarming thing about the paper was its provenance. He had seen a stack of sheets like this before. It had the same greyish tinge of recycled paper and the same closely written script. Without a shadow of doubt it belonged to the manuscript that was scattered over Patrick Halberstaedt's desk. The architect of the collage was at work in the house – in the house belonging to Parkum's mayor.

Equipped with this knowledge, and armed with the loaded gun, Viktor raced out of the shed.

# 48

Two minutes later, he was holding the key. Halberstaedt, like Viktor, kept a spare beneath the flowerpot on the porch.

As soon as the door was unlocked, he hurried into the hallway, calling Halberstaedt's name. His instincts told him that no one was there, but he checked the house anyway, running from room to room. No sign of the mayor. He was silently praying that nothing dreadful had happened to him. He refused to believe that Halberstaedt was in league with Anna. The evidence was stacked against him – his strange behaviour on the phone, and now the alarming contents of his shed – but Viktor had known him for years. The problem was, if Halberstaedt was innocent, why had he disappeared? Alarmed, Viktor suddenly thought of Isabell. There was no telling the lengths that Anna would go to, and he hoped to goodness that she wouldn't start targeting his family and friends.

He went back to the study and marched to the desk. His shoes left a trail of muddy footprints on the beige carpet, but he didn't stop to take them off.

His gaze fell on the stack of paper next to the laptop. He wondered whether it was the work of Halberstaedt or Anna. At last he was certain that the mystery would soon be solved.

He took off his raincoat, placed the gun beside the manuscript and sat down to read the first page.

The text was handwritten and laid out like an interview. As he read the first few lines, he was overwhelmed by an extraordinary sense of déjà-vu.

> *Bunte: What was it like in the aftermath of your daughter's disappearance?*
> Larenz: Like death. Of course, I was still eating, drinking and breathing and I sometimes managed to sleep for a couple of hours at a stretch, but I wasn't living anymore. My life was over the day that Josy went missing.

He started again from the beginning and felt like pinching himself to make sure he was awake. This wasn't one of Anna's stories. It was his interview. His interview with *Bunte.*

At first he couldn't figure out how Anna could have known about it, but then he remembered that the hard drive of his laptop had been wiped. She must have seized her chance, maybe yesterday when he was asleep, and stolen his files without him knowing.

It was strange that she had copied it out by hand. She could have printed the interview instead of going to the trouble of transcribing every word. The masculine writing didn't fit with her delicate hands. *Maybe it was Halberstaedt after all.* He quickly dismissed the thought:

Halberstaedt hadn't been into his house and couldn't have interfered with his computer.

Viktor leafed hurriedly through the manuscript and discovered that Anna had copied the interview in its entirety. Every question, every answer, every last sentence was there. It was a perfect copy of his work.

He turned to the laptop. It was the same make and model as his. The screensaver vanished as soon as he touched the trackpad. He wanted, no, *needed*, to see what Anna had been working on.

He clicked on a Word document. The file belonged to him. It contained the questions from *Bunte*; in fact, it was the very same email attachment that he had been sent.

His gaze came to rest on the manuscript. Theoretically, Anna could have stolen one of his files in Berlin and swiped the data from his laptop, but his computer hadn't been tampered with until yesterday evening, and Anna had been in a terrible state. How had she managed to copy the interview so quickly and with such a steady hand?

*It doesn't seem possible.*

He remembered their first encounter. Anna had come in from the beach without a trace of sand or dirt on her elegant shoes. And it had been pouring with rain.

The time factor bothered him. Was it humanly possible to fill so many pages in such a short space of time? The manuscript looked much longer than his original file.

He slid the final couple of pages from the bottom of the pile and gasped. No wonder. It wasn't his work. Anna was seriously deranged: not content with copying his answers, she had drafted her own.

He started reading:

> I feel guilty about my daughter's death. And I feel guilty about the break-up with my wife. There are plenty of things I'd do differently if I could have my time again. I shouldn't have done what I did to my wife.

He stared incredulously at the passage. Anna was obviously taking Isabell's side. Was this proof of a conspiracy? But why? What could they possibly stand to gain? Viktor had been hoping for an end to the darkness, a calming of the storm, but the manuscript was making things worse.

He was too busy reading the next passage to hear the footsteps behind him.

> I should have listened to my wife. She always knew best. Why did I accuse her of turning against me when I was the one who pushed her away? I see now that I was wrong to blame her for what happened to Josy. If only I had trusted her, Josy would be safe.

Viktor read the last sentence again and again. He couldn't make head or tail of it. Defeated, he wondered whether he should take the manuscript and leave.

But his time was up already.

# 49

'Surely you must have worked it out by now?'

Viktor recognized the voice immediately and let go of the manuscript. Panic gripped his throat like a boa constrictor. His pistol was somewhere on Halberstaedt's desk, buried under the mound of paper. He turned round and threw himself on Anna's mercy, only to discover that she was armed. She was gripping the lethal-looking carving knife so tightly that her knuckles were white. There was no doubt that she meant to hurt him, but she looked beautiful all the same. In fact, she looked as fresh and attractive as when they first met. Not a hair was out of place, her black suit, now carefully pressed, showed off her shapely figure, and her patent-leather shoes were practically sparkling in the light. She was obviously feeling much better.

*Don't try looking for me. I'LL GET TO YOU!*

Viktor decided to take the initiative and pretend not to notice her threatening stance. 'Hello there, Anna. I can help you, you know.'

*She says she's schizophrenic, but she's not.*

'Ha! You can't even help yourself! Look what you did to your own life – your daughter, your wife, your career!'

'What would you know about my wife?'

'We moved in together. She's my best friend.'

Viktor searched her face for signs of madness, but there were none. She looked prettier than ever, which added to the horror of her words.

'Would you like to tell me your real name?' he suggested, hoping to prompt a reaction.

'You know my name,' she said, still perfectly composed. 'I'm Anna. Anna Glass.'

'Fine, I'll call you Anna if you want me to, but I know the truth. The Park Clinic told me what happened.'

She smiled at him cynically. 'You checked with the clinic? I didn't realize you cared.'

'Anna Glass wasn't a patient. She was an intern – and she's dead.'

'How ghastly. How did she die?'

She turned the carving knife in her hand. The blade glinted in the light of the desk lamp, dazzling Viktor. He blinked.

'They wouldn't tell me,' he said, deciding it was safer to lie. 'Please don't do anything rash.'

His mind was racing. Years ago he had been threatened by a patient, after which a panic button had been installed beneath his desk. But the situation with Anna was far more dangerous and he had no means of calling for help. *I should have stuck to my policy of never seeing patients at home.* He decided to try a different tack.

'Didn't you say that your fictional characters tend to come alive?'

'Full marks, Dr Larenz.'

*I need to keep her talking until Halberstaedt gets home. Or until something happens – it doesn't matter what.*

It seemed expedient to play along with her so-called schizophrenia. 'When you called me earlier, you said that "she" was back. You meant one of your characters, didn't you?'

She inclined her head briefly, a gesture which Viktor interpreted as a nod.

'There's a perfectly natural explanation. You only *thought* your characters were coming to life because you transcribed my interview.'

'No,' she said firmly, shaking her head.

'You copied what I'd written, and you thought you'd made it up, but the fact is, I'm real. My daughter and I exist in real life.'

'You don't understand.'

'Anna, please! It's all quite straightforward. I'm not a figment of your imagination; I'm a normal human being. You didn't create me. The book you were working on was *my* story. I wrote it first.'

'You don't know what you're talking about!' retorted Anna, suddenly angry. She slashed the air with the carving knife. Viktor took a few steps backwards and came up against the desk.

There was an angry glint in her eyes. 'Don't you see what's happening? Surely you can't have missed the signs!'

'What signs?'

'You think you're so clever, don't you, Mr

Psychiatrist! You think I broke into your house, you think I stole your files, you think I'm in league with your wife! You even think I abducted your daughter! You don't get it, do you? You really don't get it.'

No sooner had she finished speaking than she was back to her former self – a pretty young woman dressed in quaintly conservative clothes. The cruelty and fury were gone from her face, and she smiled at him calmly. 'Never mind,' she continued, 'we're not finished yet. I'll have to take this further.'

*Further? How far is she prepared to go?*

'What do you want from me?' he asked, feeling his throat constrict with fear. He could scarcely breathe.

'Come here,' she said, jabbing the knife towards the front of the house where the windows overlooked the sea. 'I want you to take a look outside.'

Viktor followed her instructions.

'Well?' she asked.

'There's a car in the drive. A Volvo.' He spoke slowly, hesitantly, distrusting what he saw. Private vehicles were banned on Parkum and the car looked remarkably like the Volvo that was waiting for him on Sylt.

'Aren't you coming?' said Anna, who was already at the door.

'Where to?'

'I'm taking you on a little drive. We should hurry; the engine's running.'

Viktor put his face to the window and saw that someone was sitting at the wheel.

'What if I refuse to go?' he asked, looking her straight in the eye.

Without a word, Anna reached into her coat pocket and pulled out the pistol that he had been looking for on Halberstaedt's desk.

Viktor gave in to the inevitable and walked slowly to the door.

# 50

The interior of the Volvo smelt of beeswax and freshly polished leather. It was so like his own car that for a moment he was more bewildered than afraid. Three weeks ago he had left a vehicle of the same make and model in a car park on Sylt. Everything about the car was uncannily familiar, right down to the trimmings. He toyed with the idea that someone had flown his Volvo over from Sylt, but it simply wasn't possible, especially in weather like this.

'Where are you taking me?' he demanded. The question was addressed as much to the anonymous driver, who was sitting directly in front of him and looking straight ahead, as to Anna, who had taken a seat in the back.

'For a drive,' she said tersely. She clapped her hands and the driver accelerated smoothly away.

*We can't be going far*, thought Viktor. Parkum had only two roads. In six minutes they would reach the lighthouse and have to turn back.

'Where to?' he asked again.

'You know where we're going, Viktor. Work it out for yourself.'

The car picked up speed. In spite of the driving rain, the driver seemed disinclined to use his wipers.

'Read this,' said Anna, handing Viktor three closely written sheets of A4. Viktor recognized the blue biro and deduced that Anna was the author. He took the script with trepidation.

'What's this?'

'The final chapter of Charlotte's story. The conclusion. I thought you'd want to know.'

He noticed that the sheets were charred at the edges. It was almost as if Anna had turned back time and rescued the burning manuscript from the hearth.

'Read it!' ordered Anna, jabbing the pistol at the paper. He started to read.

## ON THE RUN

'Wouldn't it be easier for you to tell me what—'

'Keep reading!' she silenced him. Nervously, he read the first few lines:

The night at the Hyatt was awful. Charlotte's nose poured with blood and I had to call room service for new sheets and towels. I'd run out of tablets, but I couldn't go to the after-hours pharmacy because Charlotte was scared of being alone. After a while she dozed off. I thought about asking the porter to fetch us some penicillin and a packet of paracetamol, but it wasn't worth the risk. Charlotte was guaranteed to wake up as soon as anyone knocked on the door.

The car sped over a pothole, water spraying in all directions, and Viktor glanced up. So far the manuscript hadn't helped to explain why he was trapped in a car with a mad woman who was forcing him at gunpoint to read a handwritten account of her delusions.

*She likes to say she's schizophrenic, but she's not.*

As if the situation weren't bad enough already, the storm was still raging, visibility was down to four metres, and the driver, who was apparently deaf or dumb or both, seemed intent on clocking up a new world record. They were travelling so fast that the view through the rain-streaked windows was a blur. Viktor had no idea where he was.

'Keep reading!' said Anna as soon as he looked up. She released the safety catch to show that she meant business.

'Calm down, Anna. I'm reading, honestly I am.'

Once again, Viktor gave in to the inevitable. And once again, it was worse than he imagined.

# 51

The next morning, after a quick breakfast, we left the hotel and drove to the station. We boarded a train and got off in Westerland where we waited for about an hour. Eventually we persuaded a weather-beaten fisherman to ferry us over to Parkum. Charlotte wouldn't tell me where we were going, but it seemed to me that she wanted to get things over with. Maybe Parkum, because of its isolation, was where it was supposed to end.

On reaching dry land, Charlotte underwent a miraculous transformation. She looked positively blooming, as if the North Sea air had done her good. As if to underscore the change, she made a point of changing her name. 'Don't call me Charlotte,' she told me. 'I use another name on my little island.'

'Josy?' said Viktor, looking up.

Anna smiled at him. 'Of course. Don't tell me you didn't know already.'

'But it makes no sense. People would have noticed if you and Josy had visited Parkum. Someone would have said.'

'Of course they would,' said Anna, looking at him as if he were a feeble-minded patient who needed constant assistance. 'Keep reading.'

Viktor read on.

# 52

We followed a track to a cottage on the beach. It was a ten-minute walk from the village and the marina. Josy told me that the cottage belonged to her parents: at weekends they went to Sacrow, but in the summer and during longer breaks they holidayed on Parkum.

I was anxious to light the fire and make some tea, but Josy had other ideas.

'Come on, Anna,' she said, tugging my hand and pulling me towards the front window which afforded a spectacular view of the sea. 'It's time for the final clue.' She pointed outside. 'Look, do you see it? It was following us all the time. From Sacrow to Berlin, Berlin to Hamburg, Hamburg to Sylt – and now here. It's on the island.'

It took me a while to realize what she meant, but then I spotted a tiny figure five hundred metres from the house.

I desperately wanted to be proven wrong, but as the figure drew closer, I couldn't ignore the evidence before my eyes. Josy had been telling the truth: the evil had lived with her in Schwa-nenwerder, and it had followed us to the cottage.

I grabbed her hand and rushed to the door. I didn't know where to take her, but I knew we had to hide. A few metres from the porch was a garden shed where the generator was housed. We darted inside.

The cold, stale air clung to us like the smell of old tobacco in a telephone box, but anything was preferable to waiting in the open. I slammed the door – just in time.

By now only a hundred metres separated us from the woman on the beach.

Isabell was heading straight for the porch.

Viktor couldn't bring himself to look Anna in the eye. 'You were hiding from my wife?'

'Yes.'

'What had she done to Josy?'

'You'll find out if you keep reading.'

The roar of the Volvo's engine almost drowned out the deafening pulsing of blood in Viktor's ears. He could feel the adrenalin pumping through his body, brought on by the cocked pistol or by the speed with which they were racing down the unsealed road – or perhaps by both. He was surprised that he could think, let alone read, when his life was in the balance. *Thank God I don't get carsick,* he thought, only to chastise himself a moment later for wasting time on such trivial concerns.

He kept reading.

# 53

To my dismay, I realized that the door to the shed could only be locked from outside. At that point in time, I didn't know what Isabell was planning, the power she had over us, and what she had in store for Josy, but it was obvious that she would find us in the shed. The door was our only way out, there weren't any windows, and Isabell would be able to spot us at a glance. I thought about hiding behind the generator, but there wasn't enough space between the engine and the corrugated-iron wall. Luckily it was so noisy that we didn't have to worry about being heard.

'What did Isabell do to you?' I asked Josy while I looked for a way out of our predicament.

'I can't read the clues for you.' This time she didn't sound so sure of herself.

'I haven't got time for this,' I told her bluntly. 'If you want me to help you, I need to know what we're up against. Just tell me what she did to you.'

Josy lowered her voice to a whisper. 'She poisoned me.'

I whirled round, convinced that someone was nearing the shed.

'Why?' I asked, creeping towards the door.

'I did something wrong. She got angry with me in Sacrow.'

'What did you do?'

'I bled on the floor. Mummy didn't like it. She said I was her little girl. She doesn't want me to grow up.'

Viktor let go of the manuscript. It landed on the floor by his feet.

'Now do you see?' asked Anna.

'I think so,' he murmured.

Suddenly it all made sense. The blood in the bathroom, the poison, Isabell. But it seemed so unreal. Had Isabell wanted to punish her child for growing up? Had she tried to make Josy helpless and dependent? Was she twisted enough to poison her daughter?

'What do you know about my family?' demanded Viktor. 'Why were you involved?'

'I can't tell you,' said Anna. 'It's in the story. You'll have to keep reading.'

Viktor reached down and scrabbled in the footwell for the final pages of script. He needed to get to the end of the nightmare that he had been living for the past four years.

# 54

I opened the door an inch or two and recoiled. Isabell was standing on the porch, armed with a carving knife from the kitchen. Her gaze swept the garden, then she slowly descended from the porch.

I closed the door. 'How did she poison you?'

'I've got an allergy,' said Josy in a hoarse voice. 'Paraceta-mol and penicillin make me ill. She's the only one who knows.'

I couldn't question her any further because we were running out of time. I knew she was counting on me to protect her from Isabell, but there was nowhere for us to hide. It was hard to see anything in the gloom and I didn't want to attract attention by turning on the light, so I pulled out my lighter and flicked it on. Normally I wouldn't go near a generator with a naked flame.

Trying not to panic, I searched the shed with Josy in tow. I had to keep hold of her in case she lost her nerve and bolted.

'It's no use, Anna,' she said softly. 'Mummy will find us and kill us. I shouldn't have made her mad.'

I carried on looking and pretended not to hear, but I was steeling myself for the door to fly open and Isabell to confront us with a knife. I could hear her calling Josy's name.

'Josy? Where are you, darling? Mummy's worried.'

Her voice was unnaturally gentle and dangerously close. Josy started to cry. Fortunately the hum of the generator drowned out the noise. My cheap plastic lighter cast a flickering halo on the ceiling, walls and floor. For the millionth time I stared at the rusty generator, and at last I found the answer. A pipe led out from the bottom-right corner of the engine towards the floor. The fuel tank!

As I suspected, the tank, like the generator, had been installed long before anyone cared about safety regulations. The tank was really just a synthetic container with a diameter of almost a metre and had been dropped into the base of the shed; its sides protruded ten or so centimetres above the floor. It was protected by a thin concrete cover. I broke the seal and tried to push aside the cover. At first I thought I wasn't strong enough, but then I tried again, this time wedging my heels against the wall and channelling my fear and desperation into moving it. It worked. I managed to create an opening forty or so centimetres across, big enough for Josy and I to squeeze inside.

'I'm not going in there,' said Josy, sidling up to me and peering into the darkness. There was a nauseating smell of old diesel.

'We don't have a choice,' I told her. 'She'll find us.'

As if to prove my point, Isabell's voice sounded from outside the shed. 'Josy? Come to mummy! Where's my good little girl?'

She was only a couple of metres from the door.

'There's nothing to be afraid of, Josy,' I told her. 'Just trust me, OK?'

She was rigid with fear, which meant I could scoop her up and lower her into the tank. It was about one and a half metres deep and the diesel came up only halfway, so there was no risk of her drowning. As soon as she was safely in the tank, I sprinted to the door and jammed an ancient garden chair under the handle. Then I took a crowbar from the wall and smashed the overhead light. Working in almost total darkness, I ruptured the pipe connecting the tank to the generator, shoved the crowbar under the concrete cover and levered it into the air. My knees were screaming for me to stop, but I kept pushing down on the crowbar and at last, after one final, monumental effort, the cover thudded to the floor between the generator and the tank.

The thought of standing in the murky fluid filled me with dread, but I tried not to think about it and climbed into the tank. Another few seconds and it would have been too late. By the time I had lowered myself in and was trying to keep my balance on the slippery base, Isabell was at the door, rattling the handle.

'Josy? Are you in there?'

The chair prevented her from opening the door, but I could tell it wouldn't be long until she forced her way in.

'She'll see us,' sobbed Josy, slipping her oil-smeared hand into mine. 'Why did you move the lid?'

'She would have spotted it hanging over the side. I thought about pulling it over us, but I'm not strong enough. We'll just have to hope that she doesn't notice it on the floor.'

I knew it was ridiculous to think that she wouldn't see us; we didn't stand a chance.

The door flew open, crashing against the side of the shed. I felt a cold draught as the wind swept into the shed and swirled across the floor to our hiding place in the tank.

'Josy?'

Isabell was evidently in the shed, but I couldn't hear her

footsteps because the drone from the generator was rising all the time.

Judging by the continuing gloom, the only light in the shed came from the fading afternoon sun, which meant Isabell didn't have a torch. I was praying that she wouldn't notice the open tank – or that she wouldn't see us in the darkness. It was obvious what would happen if she decided to light a match, but surely even Isabell wouldn't do that . . .

I instructed Josy to kneel on the bottom, and she did as I said. Only her head protruded above the oil; the rest of her body was coated in cold fuel.

Just then she coughed – not her usual sickly wheezing, but a hacking cough brought on by the toxic smell. I wanted to reassure her, but when I tried to stroke her hair, my fingers left a slurry of diesel oil on her scalp.

'Don't worry. We're going to be all right,' I whispered, but Josy was inconsolable.

By now she was shaking all over and crying uncontrollably. I put my hand over her mouth, leaving enough room for her to breathe through her nose. She bit me as hard as she could. A sharp pain stabbed through my arm, but I didn't let go. I had to keep her quiet while Isabell was in the shed.

How long did we stay like that, me standing, Josy kneeling, in the foul smelling tank? I honestly don't know. All I remember is gasping for air and holding the panicking little girl in a vice-like grip while she trembled in the darkness. Maybe a minute went past, maybe five; I had no sense of time. At some point I realized that Isabell had left. The dusky light had stopped slanting across the floor. She must have closed the door.

Relieved, I loosened my hold on the sobbing Josy.

'Daddy, I'm scared,' she whimpered.

I liked the way she called me 'daddy'; it proved I'd gained her trust.

'Me too,' I said, clasping her to my side. 'But we're OK now.'

Maybe we would have been. The worst was over and Isabell had gone.

I knew she was still nearby – probably in the cottage, looking for a torch – but we had enough time, time to climb out of the tank, run to the village, call for help . . .

Time to escape.

It didn't happen that way. Josy was too upset to keep quiet. We'd been through a terrible ordeal, she was only a child, and she couldn't stop crying. She felt trapped in the slippery, smelly tank, and it was dark down there, darker than a crypt. Her sobs turned to ear-splitting screams. I couldn't do anything to stop her. We were stuck in the tank and I couldn't calm her down. But that wasn't the real problem. What sealed our fate was a mistake I'd made before Isabell entered the shed. I should never have sabotaged the fuel pipe, but I only realized the consequences now. The generator started to stutter, then cut out completely.

That was our downfall. From then on every noise from the shed could be heard outside.

# 55

Viktor's eyes welled with tears.

His poor baby, buried alive in stinking oil. He glanced at Anna, breathed in the smell of the Volvo, and felt the hum of the engine vibrating through his body. He was back in his recurring nightmare, only this time it was real.

'What happened to her? Where is she?'

'Finish the story.'

The door flew open and this time, without the noise of the generator, I heard her footsteps on the floorboards. I was running out of options. In a few seconds Isabell would reach our hiding place, and I knew she was desperate enough to shine her lighter into the tank. There was only one thing I could do to ensure that Josy didn't give us away. I dived into the generator fuel and pulled her with me.

Diesel soaked through our clothes and clung to our bodies like a cloak of death. A sticky film of oil covered our faces, clogging our mouths, plugging our nostrils and bunging our ears. At that moment I felt like a sea eagle fighting for survival in a slick of black poison, trying to clean my soiled plumage and sinking deeper and deeper beneath the tarry waves.

My lungs were screaming for air, and more than anything I

wanted to surface, but I forced myself to stay down and maintain the pressure on Josy's head. I had no idea what was happening in the shed. I couldn't see, couldn't hear, and I was running out of strength. I waited until I couldn't last another second, then shoved Josy towards the surface and came up for air. I was half expecting to see Isabell towering over the tank, but I knew I'd done my best. I'd stayed down as long as possible, and it wasn't my fault if we'd come up too soon.

We hadn't.

It was already too late.

Josy was lying limply in my arms. I wiped the oily film from her mouth and parted her lips so she could breathe. I shook her. I wanted to give her the kiss of life, but I knew in my heart that she was gone.

I still can't be sure whether it was the shock or the oil that killed her, but one thing is certain: Isabell wasn't the murderer. It was me.

Viktor desperately wanted to shout, but his voice came out in a croak. 'That's a lie and you know it!'

'No, Viktor, it's the truth,' said Anna coldly. She sneaked a quick glance out of the passenger window.

Viktor ran a hand over his eyes. He sniffed. 'Tell me it isn't true.'

'I'm afraid I can't.'

'You made it up. You're crazy.'

'Yes, I'm afraid I am.'

'Why are you torturing me? What's the point of your lies? Josy isn't dead!'

'She's dead.'

*She says she's schizophrenic because it's easier than confronting the truth.*

The engine roared and Viktor looked up. He could see lights in the distance through the rain-streaked windscreen.

'Don't worry, it won't take much longer.' She reached for his hand.

'Who are you?' he screamed at her. 'How do you know these things?'

'I'm Anna. Anna Glass.'

'Answer the question! What's your real name? What do you want from me?'

The windscreen was awash with water because the wipers were still switched off, but Viktor could tell that the lights were getting closer. He knew exactly where he was. He and Anna were racing along a pier, heading towards the open sea.

'Tell me who you are!' he shouted. He knew he was about to die, but he felt like a schoolboy after a playground fight: wretched, tearful and snotty.

'I'm Anna Glass. I killed Josy.'

The lights were only two hundred metres away. A kilometre behind them was the beach, and ahead was the wide expanse of the cold North Sea.

'WHO ARE YOU?'

The hysterical edge to his voice was swallowed up by the roaring engine, howling wind and raging waves.

'Anna. Anna Glass. There isn't much time. You should focus on what matters. You haven't read the final page.'

Viktor shook his head and raised his hand to his nose. It was bleeding.

'Suit yourself,' she said. 'I've helped you enough already, so I may as well read you the end.'

She took the final page out of his hand.

The car continued on its inexorable path towards the sea and Anna started reading.

# 56

Josy was dead. I didn't want to believe it, but I had no choice. I clung to her fragile, lifeless body and a scream rose in my throat, collecting in my mouth and pushing against my lips, but my grief was trapped by a gag of sticky oil. There was no need to hide anymore, no need to hide from Isabell; she had got what she wanted. Josy, my constant companion over the last few days; Josy, her own daughter, was dead.

I stood up and crawled out of the tank. I opened the door, rubbed the oil from my mouth and called her name.

Quietly at first, then at the top of my voice. *Isabell.* ISABELL!

I left the shed and ran towards the porch.

ISABELL! YOU KILLED HER!

I stopped, alerted by a noise. It was coming from behind me. The floor was creaking in the shed. I turned round and saw her in the doorway. At that moment I knew what had happened: she had been there all the time. She had stayed, watching and waiting while I drowned her only child.

Slowly, I walked towards her. Because of the oil in my left eye I could barely make out her features. The distance between us was down to a few metres when my vision suddenly returned. At last I could see clearly. At last I understood.

She stretched out a hand, an oil-smeared hand, and I realized the extent of my error. From the very beginning, I had got it all wrong. And I only had myself to blame. The person in front of me wasn't Isabell. I was face to face with . . .

Viktor and Anna locked gazes just as she started to speak the fatal words. And then it happened.

The car soared through the air towards the sea and at that moment, the fog cleared and Viktor saw everything with perfect clarity.

*A radiator pipe. An overhead light. A small room.*

At last he understood.

*A metal-framed bed. A grey carpet. A drip.*

It all made sense.

Anna Glass!

The insight seared through his body and took possession of his mind.

*I was face to face with . . .*

The final piece of the jigsaw was in place: *Anna.* A-n-n-a forwards and a-n-n-A backwards. Anna in the looking glass. Anna Glass.

'I'm you,' he said. With that, the car faded from view and he found himself in a hospital room.

'Yes.'

It was the last time that the sound of his own voice would make him jump. He felt like a startled animal who had finally recognized its reflection in the mirror. He repeated the sentence to be sure that he wasn't mistaken.

'I was face to face with . . .'

'I was face to face with . . . myself.'

No one said a word.

*

It was Monday November 26, and bright winter sunshine was slanting through the bars of room 1245 where Dr Viktor Larenz, former psychiatrist and world expert on schizophrenia, was being treated for multiple psychological disorders at the renowned Wedding Psychosomatic Clinic in Berlin. After four years of treatment, the patient, who had been taken off his medication almost a fortnight earlier, was experiencing his first moment of clarity since his daughter disappeared.

The wind had dropped, the clouds were clearing and the storms that had shaken the city over the past few days had moved on. It was a crisp, sunny afternoon.

# 57

*Nine days later, Berlin-Wedding Psychosomatic Clinic*

The lecture theatre was unusually empty. At the lectern, a small grey-haired character was holding forth to two men sat opposite him in the middle of the front row, surrounded by empty chairs. Most of the auditorium, which seated five hundred, was steeped in darkness, but a row of spotlights illuminated the stage. Contrary to normal practice, the doors to the theatre were locked.

Professor Malzius, the clinic's director, was in the process of communicating highly sensitive information to Freymann and Lahnen, two of the best defence lawyers in Berlin.

'Prior to his breakdown, Dr Larenz was an eminent psychiatrist with a successful clinic in central Berlin. I'm sure you're both aware of his myriad achievements, so I won't review them in detail now. Suffice to say, he was the author of numerous books and a regular guest on radio and TV.'

The lawyers nodded and cleared their throats. Professor Malzius reached for the remote control and pointed it at the projector. They saw a portrait photo of a striking young doctor in his office, then the next slide appeared. It was still recognizably Dr Larenz, but this time in a lamentable state, curled up naked in a foetal position on a hospital bed.

'He suffered a nervous breakdown following the disappearance of his daughter. He was admitted to the clinic on a temporary basis, but his condition worsened and he never recovered sufficiently to be transferred or released.'

He clicked to another slide. It was a newspaper headline:

## STILL SEARCHING FOR JOSY
**Four Years Since Celebrity Psychiatrist's Daughter Vanished Without Trace**

'Four years ago last November, Dr Larenz's twelve-year-old daughter went missing. In the eleven months preceding her disappearance she developed a range of inexplicable symptoms. The cause of her illness, the nature of her abduction and the identity of those responsible remained a mystery...' explained Malzius. He paused for a few seconds. '...Until now!'

He was interrupted by one of the lawyers, a small man with curly blonde hair, who shot to his feet as if to say *Objection, your Honour!*

'With all due respect, Professor Malzius, my colleague and I were hoping to hear something new. We're running out of time.'

'Thank you, Mr Lahnen. I'm aware that you and Mr Freymann have an extremely busy schedule.'

'Good. In that case you'll understand our concern. Our client is scheduled for transfer to the psychiatric wing of Moabit penitentiary in precisely thirty minutes. The preliminary hearing takes place tomorrow, which means we need to consult with our client today. Once he's released from this facility, the law will deem him well enough to stand trial for manslaughter or possibly murder.'

'Indeed,' snapped Malzius, irritated at being interrupted in his own auditorium by someone without a medical degree. 'If you'll allow me to proceed with the briefing, you may find yourself learning something of relevance to his defence.'

Lahnen pursed his lips and sat back down.

'For four years the patient was unaware of his surroundings,' continued Malzius. 'He was living in an imaginary world, disconnected from reality. Then three weeks ago we took a radical, and dare I say *groundbreaking* step with regard to his treatment. I'll spare you the medical details and focus on the results.'

Lahnen and Freymann nodded gratefully.

'The first thing to understand is that Viktor Larenz suffers from two distinct conditions: Munchausen syndrome by proxy and schizophrenia. I assume you're more familiar with the latter, so I'll acquaint you with Munchausen's first. The syndrome derives its name from the notoriously boastful Baron Munchausen. Its sufferers lie about their health in order to gain sympathy from medical professionals and friends. By feigning physical symptoms, patients have been known to convince their doctors to carry out unnecessary surgery – appendicectomies, for example. They may also attempt to prolong the need for treatment by rubbing excrement or vomit into a wound.'

'That's crazy,' muttered Lahnen, frowning. His colleague looked similarly appalled.

'Well yes, they're mentally unwell. The trouble is, diagnosis is very difficult. Munchausen's is more common than most people realize. Video surveillance has been used in some hospitals to help with detection, but it wouldn't have picked up on Larenz's problem. You see, Larenz suffered from Munchausen's by proxy, aka fabricated or induced illness or FII, which means he inflicted symptoms on someone else, namely his daughter.'

Malzius paused to measure the effect of his words.

'Larenz alone was aware that his daughter suffered from an immune system disorder, and he used his medical knowledge to murderous effect. Josephine, or Josy as he called her, had a hypersensitive reaction to paracetamol and penicillin, both of which he administered in increasing quantities. I suppose you could say it was the perfect crime. Larenz continued to prescribe paracetamol for Josephine's headaches and penicillin for her other mysterious symptoms, and everyone thought he was an exemplary father. His family and friends knew nothing of her allergies, so the regimen of drugs seemed medically sound. As it happened, Larenz was putting his daughter into anaphylactic shock. During the final stages, the doses were high enough to kill her.'

The clinic director broke off to take a sip of water.

'The endless round of doctor's appointments and consultations is another typical symptom of FII. In Larenz's case, the abusive behaviour was triggered by an incident that occurred when he, his wife and his daughter were on holiday in Sacrow. Josephine was eleven years old at the time and the father–daughter relationship was extremely close. All that was about to change. Josephine needed more privacy: she started closeting herself in the bathroom and she seemed more at ease in the company of her mother. There was a simple explanation: she had started to menstruate. Larenz was devastated by this milestone in his daughter's development. He couldn't cope with the idea that his little girl would soon become an independent adult. Not even his wife had noticed his pathologically possessive attitude to Josephine and so it didn't occur to her that he would deliberately poison their daughter to stop her growing up. He administered paracetamol and penicillin to make her vulnerable and dependent – typical FII. The syndrome is usually associated with mothers. It's the first time I've seen it in a male.'

'Fascinating, Professor Malzius,' said Freymann, seizing his chance. 'Perhaps we could focus on the legal aspect. In your opinion, was Dr Larenz responsible for his actions? He poisoned his daughter over a period of nearly a year. That involves planning and premeditation, does it not?'

'Not necessarily. Larenz is a pathological liar. He suffers from FII and he lied about his daughter's illness, but it's more complicated than that. Larenz *believes* his lies; he's delusional. And so we come to his second disorder: schizophrenia.'

Malzius looked from Freymann to Lahnen.

'His behaviour doesn't follow the usual rules.'

# 58

The doors to the auditorium were locked, so Dr Roth was obliged to brave the cold and peer through the outside windows. A few minutes earlier, Viktor had reached the end of his story, and Roth had hurried downstairs to find out where the lawyers had got to. He was secretly hoping that the professor was treating his visitors to one of his famously long-winded explanations: the usual difficulty was persuading him to stop. The lights in the auditorium were still dimmed and Malzius was in full flow. In fact, judging by the number of slides remaining, he and the lawyers would be busy for at least another fifteen minutes, enough time for Roth to achieve what he had to, provided that he was quick. He set off determinedly, stopping at the onsite pharmacy to collect some tablets, and arrived three minutes later at Viktor's door. He paused for a moment to recover his breath, smooth his hair and peer through the spyhole: no change. Viktor, still tied to the bed, was staring at the ceiling. Roth hovered outside, then made up his mind and inserted the cumbersome key into the lock. A quick turn to the right, and the metal door sprang open.

'So you're back.'

Viktor raised his head a little and craned his neck to see the psychiatrist walk into the room. Roth's left hand was thrust deep into his pocket, so Viktor couldn't be certain whether he was carrying anything or not.

'Yes, I'm back.'

'Have you decided to help me after all?'

Dr Roth strode wordlessly to the window and gazed into the darkness. It had been snowing since early that morning, and the flakes had settled, covering the ugly concrete forecourt in a blanket of snow.

'Have you got what I asked for?'

'I'm still not—'

'Come on, Dr Roth, you heard what happened, and you know that I'm right.'

Privately, Roth agreed, but he didn't want to put his career on the line without reminding Viktor of the risk he was taking on his behalf. He hesitated.

'I'm counting on you, Dr Roth. We don't have much time. They're already half an hour late.'

'All right, Dr Larenz, I must be mad to agree to this, but I'll do as you ask. You trusted me with your story, and after this we'll be quits. Don't ask me to do anything more.'

Roth left the jar of pills in his pocket, withdrew his left hand and deftly loosened the straps. Viktor rubbed his wrists and ankles gratefully. 'Thanks. That was kind of you.'

'No problem. Look, we've got ten minutes at most,

then I need you back in the restraints. Do you want to go to the bathroom and freshen up?'

'No. You know what I want.'

'You want your freedom.'

'Yes.'

'Out of the question. You know I can't do it.'

'Why? I thought once you'd heard the full story—'

'Have I heard the full story?'

'Of course. I told you everything.'

'I'm not convinced you did.' Dr Roth shook his head and breathed out heavily through his nostrils. 'I think you're hiding something. Something important. You know what I'm talking about, don't you?'

'Do I?' said Viktor with a roguish smile.

'What's so funny?'

'Nothing.' Viktor grinned. 'I was wondering how long it would take you to ask.'

# 59

Professor Malzius cleared his throat, took another sip of water and continued his lecture in the monotonous drone otherwise reserved for those who had the dubious pleasure of being a doctor, patient or student at the clinic.

'Larenz's schizophrenia allowed him to inhabit a different reality. In the early stages of his condition, he was anchored in the normal world, but after a while the delusions became his life. Because of his schizophrenia, he wasn't aware of what he was doing to his daughter. It was a kind of defence mechanism: the delusions allowed him to continue administering paracetamol and penicillin in the belief that Josephine needed the medication. He didn't have to pretend to be a devoted father, he truly believed it, and everything he did was geared towards making her better: he gave up his job and threw himself into the search for a cure. Josephine was seen by every imaginable specialist – with one glaring exception: Larenz omitted to take her to an allergist. As Josephine's condition worsened, so too did his delusions. His relationship with Isabell deteriorated and he persuaded himself that she was to blame for Josephine's ill health. In fact, he even went so far as to accuse her of killing his daughter, when all the while he was the culprit, albeit without knowing it.'

'In other words, manslaughter, not murder,' broke in Freymann, a thickset giant of a man. He was wearing a double-breasted navy blazer with distinctive buttons. A gold chain led from his belt to the timepiece in his pocket, and a paunch had started to form above the waistband of his grey trousers.

'The legal ramifications are your concern,' said Malzius, taking a tone more commonly used with ill-mannered children. 'My task, as I understand it, is to outline the facts – and those are the facts, to the best of our knowledge. But if you want my opinion, Dr Larenz can't be held responsible for what he did. He certainly didn't intend to kill his daughter; he only wanted to stop her growing up. And it wasn't premeditated: Josephine didn't die because of the poison; she drowned.'

He reached for the remote control and forwarded to the next slide. It showed the Larenzs' villa in Schwanenwerder.

'Dr Larenz's house – a truly magnificent place.'

Freymann and Lahnen shifted in their seats and nodded impatiently.

'At the time of the accident, Larenz's schizophrenia had reached an advanced stage. He believed that he and his daughter were on holiday on a small North Sea island called Parkum, when actually they were in the garden at home. The fateful hallucinations began when he became convinced that Isabell, who was at work that day as usual, was at the front door. As I mentioned before, he already perceived Isabell as a threat to his daughter and, on hearing her voice, he picked up Josephine and took her to the boathouse.'

Malzius pressed the remote control and pointed to an attractive wooden building on the water's edge.

'By this stage he had persuaded himself that Isabell intended to harm them, so he told his daughter to keep quiet and hide. Josephine was understandably alarmed and started to scream. Larenz responded by putting his hand over her mouth and pushing her under the water. Unfortunately, she drowned.'

Malzius looked up and saw the two lawyers whispering and muttering. He could make out isolated words such as 'paragraph 20' and 'psychiatric care'.

'If I could have your attention for a moment,' he interrupted them. 'As you know, I'm not a lawyer, but I understand the verdict will hinge on whether Larenz intended to kill his daughter.'

'To some extent, yes.'

'The question of intent can be settled with reference to one obvious fact: Larenz loved his daughter with all his heart. As soon as he realized what he had done, he experienced a second psychotic episode. He desperately wanted to undo the damage: to make his daughter well again, to bring her back to life. In his delusional state, he believed that she was still with him. He bundled her into the car and went to see an allergist. The clinic was so busy that no one noticed he was alone. There was no record of an appointment, but the mix-up was blamed on the new receptionist who was struggling to learn the ropes. After a while, Larenz left the waiting room to fetch a glass of water, came back and started claiming that Josephine had been abducted. Dr Grohlke, the allergist, was a family friend, and neither he nor the police had any reason to doubt Larenz's story. Before he could leave the clinic, Larenz broke down and was admitted to our care. For four years, he failed to respond to treatment. Naturally we assumed that the illness had been prompted by the stress of Josephine's disappearance, and we medicated him accordingly. Contrary to our expectations, the regimen didn't work. In fact, it had the opposite effect: with every day, the likelihood of a recovery seemed more remote. Of course, had we known that Larenz had killed his daughter, we would have handled the matter quite differently. As it was, we treated him for depression, and the medication made him worse. For most of his time here, he was in a state of catatonic paralysis, unable to speak or move. Unknown to us, he was living in a make-believe world on the island of Parkum, surrounded by imaginary characters including a dog named Sindbad, a mayor named Halberstaedt and a ferryman called Burg. He believed he was working on an interview. Needless to say, it was a delusion.'

'What makes you think that he's fit to stand trial?' demanded Freymann, worried that they were running out of time. He glanced at his pocket watch. 'Larenz was seriously ill. For four years he lived in an imaginary world. You said on the phone that he was well enough to talk to us. What changed?'

'I'm glad you asked,' said Malzius. 'Let's take a look at these slides.' He inserted a new cartridge into the projector.

'Consider the progression of his illness. Here he is on the day he was admitted. As you can see, he's confused, but he's looking at the camera. From then on he deteriorated.' The images changed in quick succession. 'During the final stages he broke down completely. Here you see him lying in his room, drooling and staring blankly at the walls.'

Malzius cleared his throat. 'Even as laymen, I'm sure you can see that our attempts to treat him were making him worse. The medication, the attempts at therapy – nothing seemed to work. Then one of our young psychiatrists, Dr Martin Roth, suggested a new approach to the case. Frankly, the idea was somewhat unorthodox, but we gave it a go. We stopped Larenz's meds.'

'Aha,' said Lahnen excitedly. 'And once he was off the drugs—'

'—the self-healing process could begin,' continued Malzius, cutting him off. 'His delusions continued, but this time they centred around an imaginary therapist: Anna Glass.'

Lahnen gave a low whistle and was reprimanded with a glare from his colleague. They were both big shots in the legal world, but Freymann was obviously the senior of the two.

'Larenz initially mistook Anna for a patient, but he eventually learned the truth: he was the patient and she was his analyst. The clue was in her name: like a looking glass, she reflected his behaviour and showed him what he had done. At last he was able to come to terms with the death of his daughter, which makes him the first schizophrenic patient to treat his own disorder with the help of his delusions.'

The lights went on. The lecture, as the lawyers realized to their relief, was finally at an end. They were an hour behind schedule and a written report would have done just as well. But the time hadn't been entirely wasted: they had gleaned a number of useful details that would help with their client's defence.

'Is there anything else I can help you with?' enquired the professor, unlocking the doors and ushering his listeners into the foyer.

'Actually, there is,' said Freymann, while Lahnen nodded vigorously in the background.

'Your report was most interesting, but . . .'

'But what?' snapped Professor Malzius, raising his eyebrows in disapproval. He hadn't reckoned with anything but praise.

'Our present understanding of events derives from information provided by the patient after he recovered from his catatonic state. Isn't that so?'

Malzius nodded. 'More or less. He hasn't been

especially forthcoming. We had to piece together the facts.'

The professor had told them over the phone that Larenz had been particularly guarded over the past few days, refusing to speak to anyone apart from Dr Roth. Not surprisingly, it was impossible to say for certain what had been running through Larenz's head on the day that Josephine died.

Freymann wasn't satisfied. 'You said yourself that Dr Larenz is a pathological liar. What makes you think that his latest story isn't a fabrication?'

Malzius, who considered the question a waste of his time, looked from his watch to the digital clock on the wall and back to his watch. 'I don't think you understand the nature of psychiatry,' he said tetchily. 'When can we ever be sure? But in my considered opinion, it's highly unlikely that a Munchausen patient would simulate a schizophrenic episode lasting four years in order to lend credence to a lie. Now if there's nothing else, I suggest you—'

'No!' snapped Freymann, raising his voice ever so slightly. His tone wasn't exactly rude, but it was enough to stop Malzius in his tracks.

'Is there a problem?' asked the professor, visibly annoyed.

'Just one last question.'

Malzius frowned and shifted his gaze from Freymann to Lahnen and back again.

'What?' he demanded. 'Wasn't my briefing sufficiently thorough?'

'You didn't answer the real question. The question that brings us here.' Freymann smiled innocently. 'Where's the corpse?'

# 60

'Bravo!' said Viktor, clapping his frail hands. 'An obvious question, but well done for asking all the same.'

'So where is it, then?' persisted Dr Roth. 'What did you do with the body?'

Viktor stopped clapping, rubbed his wrists and stared at the floor. The strip lighting gave the brown linoleum a greenish tinge. 'Very well,' he sighed. 'But I want to make a deal.'

'You tell me the end of the story, and I'll give you your freedom?'

'Yes.'

'I'm sorry but I can't!'

Viktor expelled a long breath of air. 'I know I deserve to be punished. I did the worst thing a father could do. I loved my daughter more than anything in the world, and I killed her. I killed my own child. But I wasn't well; I'm still not well, and I never will be. What will happen if they put me on trial? The media will have a field day, I'll be locked away for the rest of my life, or sectioned if I'm lucky, but will the world be any better for my imprisonment?'

Dr Roth shrugged.

'My point is: how would society benefit? Yes, I committed a murder, but I'm not a violent man. You could release me right now in the knowledge that I'd never hurt anyone again. Why? Because I could never love anyone as much as I loved Josy. Don't you think I've been punished enough? Putting me on trial won't be in anyone's interest.'

Roth shook his head. 'Perhaps not, but what do you expect me to do? I'd be breaking the law.'

'Good heavens, Dr Roth, I'm not asking you to unlock the door. You don't have to worry about me escaping in the literal sense. Just give me my meds and I'll go back to Parkum.'

'To Parkum? After everything you've told me about the place? Parkum was a nightmare!'

'Parkum only became a nightmare when you stopped my medication. Before that, it was the island of my dreams.' Viktor chuckled at his own choice of words. 'The sun was out, Halberstaedt took care of the generator, Michael brought me fresh fish, Sindbad dozed at my feet, and my wife called every day – she was hoping to join me as soon as she could. But best of all, Josy was with me. Everything was perfect. The storm gathered later.'

Deep down, Roth wanted to help him. He reached into his pocket and wrapped his fingers around the bottle of pills. 'I don't know. It wouldn't be ethical.'

'OK,' said Viktor, sitting up in bed. 'Here's your

incentive. I'll answer your question, but on one condition – you give me my tablets first.'

'No,' replied Roth, smoothing the hair nervously over his temples. 'You tell me what happened to her body, and I'll give you the meds.'

'Don't I deserve a bit of trust? I told you my story without the promise of anything in return. Now it's your turn. Give me the tablets and I'll tell you where to look. You won't notice any change for a couple of minutes. You'll have more than enough time to find out what you want to know.'

Dr Roth hovered uncertainly at his bedside. What he was doing contradicted everything he stood for as a doctor. But he couldn't help himself; he simply had to know.

He withdrew his hand from his pocket and took out a small plastic bottle of pills containing the medication that Viktor had received in the form of an injection every day throughout his stay at the clinic – with the exception of the last three weeks.

'Thank you.' Viktor immediately counted out eight tablets and placed them on the palm of his unnaturally pallid hand. Roth watched impassively, but as soon as the pills were in Viktor's mouth, he was seized with an urge to take them back. But it was already too late; Viktor had swallowed them.

'Relax, Dr Roth, I intend to keep my promise. You made the right choice. And, anyway, it's been exactly three weeks – isn't it time I had a relapse? No one will think to do a blood test – and my lawyers will see to it that no one tries. It's their job to keep me out of the dock. Professor Malzius will find me staring blankly at the ceiling, and he'll lose his confidence in my powers of self-healing. He wasn't comfortable about stopping the meds in the first place – he'll go back to pumping me full of drugs.'

'What if he decides to have your stomach pumped?'

'That's a risk I'm prepared to live, or die, with.' Viktor fell back against his pillows. He had doubled his standard dosage and the effects were evident in his laboured breathing and stilted speech. He raised a weary hand and beckoned for Dr Roth to approach. The psychiatrist bent down so that Viktor could whisper in his ear.

It came as a shock to see his patient's unsteady gaze. Fearing that he was about to lose the answer to his question, he took Viktor by the shoulders and gave him a shake. 'Where's Josy?' he demanded. 'What did you do with her body?'

Viktor's eyelids flickered, then he focused and looked the psychiatrist in the eye. When he spoke, his voice was steady and determined.

'Listen carefully,' he said.

Dr Roth bent even closer, as close as he could get.

'Pay attention to what I tell you. It will make your career.'

# Epilogue

*Six months later, Côte d'Azur*

Suite 910 of the Vista Palace Hotel in Roquebrune commanded spectacular views of Cape Martin and Monaco, but that was only part of its appeal. In addition to three bedrooms and two bathrooms, the luxury apartment came with a private pool to save its well-to-do inhabitants the indignity of swimming with the riff-raff who could only afford an executive room.

Isabell Larenz was relaxing on a lounger by the pool. Rather than eat in the restaurant, she had availed herself of the twenty-four-hour room service and ordered a fillet steak with Italian potatoes and a glass of champagne. A white-liveried waiter had brought the meal on a silver platter and was serving it on a porcelain plate. A second waiter had gone inside to find a chair to match the teak dining table. Isabell had no intention of making do with ordinary garden furniture.

'Madam, someone is at the door.'

'I beg your pardon?'

Annoyed at the interruption, Isabell put down the

latest edition of *InStyle* magazine and shaded her eyes with her hand.

'Madam, there's a gentleman to see you. Would you like me to show him in?'

'I suppose so,' she said, standing up and signalling impatiently for him to get on with it. She was hungry, the waiters had outstayed their welcome, and she was looking forward to her lunch. While she waited, she dipped her big toe into the pool and looked critically at her nails: it was time for the hotel's beauty therapist to pay another visit to her suite. Yesterday's choice of nail varnish would look dreadful with the outfit she was planning to wear tonight.

'Good afternoon, Mrs Larenz.'

Groaning inwardly, Isabell turned round and saw a stranger standing in the sliding doors to the lounge. He was of medium height, his hair was tousled and he was neatly, but not expensively, dressed.

'Who are you?' she demanded, wondering where the waiters had gone. They usually hung around for a tip, but this time they had disappeared without dishing up the vegetables. She tutted in displeasure.

'My name is Roth, Dr Martin Roth. I'm your husband's doctor.'

'I see,' said Isabell. She couldn't sit down and start eating without asking her visitor to join her, so she hovered uncertainly by the pool.

'I'm here with an important message, something your husband told me before he suffered his last relapse.'

'Why the urgency? Surely you haven't flown here from Berlin to pass on a message? Couldn't you have called?'

'It's something we should probably discuss in person.'

'Very well, Dr Roth. It seems like a fuss about nothing, but if you insist.' She gestured to the chair with feigned politeness. 'Would you like to take a seat?'

'No thanks, it won't take long.' Dr Roth strolled across the patio, stopped in the middle of the lawn, and positioned himself in the sun. 'Beautiful apartment.'

'Yes.'

'Have you stayed here before?'

'I haven't visited Europe in over four years ... Look, I know you've come a long way, but could we get this over with quickly? My lunch is getting cold.'

'You moved to Buenos Aires, didn't you?' persisted Roth as if he hadn't heard. 'You left Berlin after Josy passed away.'

'I needed to get away. Anyone with children would understand.'

'Indeed.' He looked at her intently. 'Mrs Larenz, your husband confessed to inducing an allergic reaction in your daughter over a period of eleven months. He also admitted to drowning her accidentally.'

'The lawyers I hired acquainted me with the facts.'

'In that case, they probably told you that his confession triggered a serious relapse.'

'Yes, he hasn't shown any sign of recovery, as far as I'm aware.'

'But I don't suppose they mentioned the subject of our last conversation. In the final moments before Viktor returned to his state of catatonic paralysis, he agreed to tell me what happened to the body.'

Isabell showed no visible sign of emotion. She reached for the Gucci sunglasses perching on her head and lowered them over her eyes.

'Well?' she said steadily. 'What did he say?'

'We know where she is.'

'Where?' she asked.

Roth, who had been studying her face intently, detected the first sign of emotion. Her lower lip was trembling. He crossed the lawn and leant over the railings. The hotel was situated at the top of a bluff, several hundred metres above the sea.

'Come and join me,' he said encouragingly.

'Why?'

'Please, Mrs Larenz, this isn't easy for me. I'd rather tell you here.'

Isabell hesitated, then joined him at the railings.

'Do you see the main pool?' asked Roth, pointing to the terrace diagonally below them.

'Yes.'

'Why don't you swim there?'

'For heaven's sake, Dr Roth, I've got my own pool. And quite frankly, I'd rather we stuck to the matter at hand.'

'Of course,' he murmured without looking up. He

seemed to be staring at the people in the pool. 'The thing is, I've been trying to work out what that gentleman is doing there.' He pointed to a well-toned figure in red-and-white trunks. The man, who must have been in his early forties, was dragging his lounger into the shade.

'How should I know? We've never met.'

'He lives in the suite next door. Like me, he's a member of the medical profession, and like you, he paid for an apartment with a pool ... But he never seems to use it.'

'I'm beginning to lose my patience, Dr Roth. I thought you wanted to tell me what happened to my daughter, not to cast aspersions on the bathing habits of people who needn't concern us.'

'Absolutely. I apologize. It's just ...'

'What?' snapped Isabell, removing her sunglasses and glaring at him with her jet-black eyes.

'Well, maybe he prefers the main pool because it gives him a chance to eye up the girls. He seems to like the look of that pretty teenager. Blonde hair, three loungers to the left, not far from the shower.'

'That's it,' snapped Isabell. 'I've got no interest whatsoever in your—'

'Oh really?' Dr Roth put two fingers in his mouth and let out a shrill whistle.

The noise attracted the attention of a number of people around the pool, including the fair-haired girl. She put down her book. On seeing Dr Roth waving, she returned the greeting.

'*Hola?*' she called hesitantly, getting up and taking a few steps back from the lounger to get a better look.

Isabell froze as the girl stared first at Dr Roth, then at her.

'*Hola. Qué pasa?*' she shouted in Spanish. '*Quién es el hombre, mami?*'

Isabell, as predicted by Dr Roth, immediately tried to flee. She got as far as the patio doors before a man burst into the apartment.

'Isabell Larenz, I'm arresting you on suspicion of perverting the course of justice, and for criminal negligence,' said the French official.

'That's ridiculous,' she protested.

The handcuffs snapped shut.

'You'll regret this!'

The policeman muttered something into his walkie-talkie and seconds later a helicopter thudded into view, approaching the hotel from a distance of a hundred or so metres.

'No one could fault your ingenuity, Mrs Larenz,' said Roth, following the policeman outside. Isabell kept walking but he knew she was listening.

'Josy didn't drown. She was unconscious when you found her. You smuggled her out of Berlin and put her on a boat to South America. Viktor's schizophrenia made him suggestible, and you encouraged him to believe that Josy was dead. Naturally, he broke down when he thought he had killed her. After that, you had power of attorney and could claim his fortune for yourself. Your lawyers took care of the paperwork, and there was enough money in the bank to silence the rumours about the psychiatrist's wife and her little girl – that's the advantage of Argentina, I suppose. It worked nicely for four years, but you made a mistake. You were wrong to bring Josy back to Europe. After Viktor's confession, you thought you were safe.'

The police officer frogmarched Isabell up the stairs to the fifth floor and escorted her on to the roof of the Vista Palace Hotel. The helicopter pad had been intended for use by affluent guests, but it was currently occupied by a military chopper belonging to the French police. Isabell maintained a stony silence and paid no attention to the questions shouted after her by Dr Roth.

'What did you tell Josy? Did you persuade her that she'd be better off in Buenos Aires without the media watching her every move? How did she like her new identity? Does she ask to see her father?'

Isabell didn't reply. She showed no interest in answering his questions – or in asking any of her own. Most people would have demanded a lawyer or begged for the right to say goodbye to the teenager who was being comforted by a policewoman on the poolside below. Isabell said nothing and was marched away without a fight.

'Your husband was ill,' shouted Dr Roth, hoping that his voice wasn't being drowned out by the helicopter blades. 'But you . . . you're just mercenary.'

At last Isabell stopped and turned. The policeman

immediately drew his gun. Isabell seemed to be saying something, but Roth couldn't hear what. He took a step closer.

'How did Viktor find out?'

The words reached him loud and clear.

'How did my husband find out?'

*Oh he knew straightaway*, thought Roth without replying. Viktor had known as soon as his head cleared and he was able to think. He had known long before Roth asked him about the body. The police had discovered no evidence of Josy's corpse in the boathouse, and so Viktor had concluded that his daughter wasn't dead. And if Josy wasn't dead, someone must have spirited her away. It wasn't hard to do the maths.

Viktor's insistence on returning to Parkum had puzzled Roth at first. But then he realized that his patient had wanted to retreat from reality precisely *because* his daughter was alive. He was afraid. Horribly afraid. Afraid of what he might do to his daughter. He had hurt her, almost killed her. His illness was incurable, and as a psychiatrist, he was well aware of that. And so he had chosen the only place where Josy would be safe from him: Parkum.

'How did Viktor find out?' repeated Isabell, struggling to make herself heard above the din of the thudding blades.

'*She* told him,' shouted Roth. For a moment he was surprised to hear himself saying exactly what Viktor would have wanted his wife to hear.

'Told him? *Who* told him?'

'Anna.'

'Anna?'

The policeman gave Isabell a little shove and ordered her to keep moving. She stumbled forward but kept looking back. She wanted to talk to Dr Roth, to ask a final question. But she was moving away from him and he couldn't make out the words. He didn't need to. He could read her question from the movement of her lips.

'Who the hell is Anna?'

Her uncomprehending expression, the helplessness in her eyes as the helicopter took off, was the last that Martin Roth saw of her. It was an image he never forgot.

Slowly, he turned and headed for the stairs. As he made his way down, he knew that the real challenge lay ahead. In the coming months he would face the first true test of his ability as a therapist. A new patient was waiting for him and it was his job to break the truth to her. He had given her father his word.

# Acknowledgements

First and foremost, I'd like to thank you, the reader. Not because I have to, but because I think we share a certain solidarity. Reading and writing are solitary and intensely personal activities, and I'm honoured to be the recipient of the most valuable gift in the world: your time. Especially if you've made it all the way through to these acknowledgements.

Maybe you'd like to tell me what you thought of the book. You can contact me via my website:
www.sebastianfitzek.de

Or send me an email:
fitzek@sebastianfitzek.de

Next I'd like to thank all the people who had a hand in 'creating' me, for example:

My literary agent, Roman Hocke, who treated me like one of his many bestselling authors and never made me feel like a novice.

My UK agent Tanja Howarth who opened the doors to Pan Macmillan where I was given the warmest of welcomes by Stefanie Bierwerth and Daniela Rapp, my editors in London and New York. Thank you for all your hard work in making a dream come true and getting a first-time novelist from Berlin published in the language of his literary heroes, the world's greatest thriller writers.

My translator, Sally-Ann Spencer, who did such a thorough and wonderful job with the English edition that I like the book even better than before.

My German editor, Dr Andrea M. Müller, who 'discovered' me and played a significant role in shaping the novel.

My friend Peter Prange, who unselfishly shared the lessons learnt from years of writing bestselling novels, and his wife, Serpil Prange, who offered excellent guidance and comments. They were very generous with their time, and I hope I managed to follow their advice.

Clemens, my brother, who helped with the medical content. It can never hurt to have an expert on neuroradiology in the family, and it's a relief to our parents that one of us is working in a sensible profession. To ensure that Clemens doesn't get blamed for my mistakes, I should point out that he didn't check my drafts.

Every book represents the culmination of a long journey, and mine began with my parents, Christa and Freimut Fitzek. I thank them for their love and unstinting support.

Stories are only worth telling if you've got someone to tell them to. Gerlinde deserves recognition for listening to *Therapy* in its entirety at least six times and giving each new version her enthusiastic approval. Of course, her objectivity may be somewhat in doubt.

Then there are all the people whose names I don't know but without whom this book wouldn't exist in its current form: the designers who came up with the brilliant cover, the typesetters, the printers, the booksellers who put the novel on the shelves.

And I couldn't finish these acknowledgements without thanking you, Viktor Larenz. Wherever you may be . . .

**Sebastian Fitzek,**
*the sunniest day of the year,*
*Parkum*

# ABOUT THE AUTHOR

SEBASTIAN FITZEK is one of Europe's most successful authors of psychological thrillers. His books have sold thirteen million copies, been translated into more than thirty-six languages and are the basis for international cinema and theatre adaptations. Sebastian Fitzek was the first German author to be awarded the European Prize for Criminal Literature. He lives with his family in Berlin.

Follow Sebastian on www.sebastianfitzek.com
and @sebastianfitzek on Instagram.